BEAR TRUFFLE MURDER

A MAPLE HILLS COZY MYSTERY #11

WENDY MEADOWS

MAJESTIC OWL
PUBLISHING LLC

1

The air was warming up as the sun rose over Maple Hills. Nikki was in her shop enjoying the arrival of spring. *No more bulky coats,* she thought as she took off her light jacket. June in Maple Hills brought a promise of warmth to come. Nikki was happy to have seen the last of the snow. She walked to the front of her chocolate shop and opened the door. There were no customers waiting, but Nikki was not worried. She knew the store would be busy later. Nikki had brewed some coffee, and she took advantage of the quiet to sit and enjoy a cup. A few minutes later, Tori and Lidia walked into the shop. Lidia was an older woman who worked harder than anyone Nikki knew. Tori was younger and sweet. They worked for Nikki and were reporting for duty.

"Hi, Nikki," they said together. Nikki invited them to sit and have some coffee. They both grabbed cups and sat down.

"I've been thinking," started Nikki, "It is getting too warm to run a hot chocolate shop." She and Lidia had come up with that idea in the fall. Customers had been talking about how cold it was, and the two friends came up with a solution. Now that it was warming up, Nikki thought it would be better to offer something cooler.

"How about milkshakes?" she asked the other ladies. Tori and Lidia agreed that milkshakes would be a perfect transition into the summer and warmer weather.

"We could also sell floats," Lidia suggested. Nikki and Tori agreed.

"We could make our own ice cream," Tori suggested.

"That sounds like a lot of trouble," said Nikki.

"Actually, they have some industrial ice cream makers for sale at the kitchen warehouse in the next town over," Tori said. "I noticed them last time I was there."

"I can look into an ice cream freezer," offered Lidia. Lidia had lived in Maple Hills all her life. She had connections in the town. *If you need it, ask Lidia*, thought Nikki.

"Okay," Nikki agreed. "Let's look into it."

Tori said she would call the kitchen warehouse, and Lidia said she would call some friends. While they were making their calls, a customer walked in. Nikki recognized him and asked if he needed some chocolates. He said yes, and she went to the counter to help him. He was a local teacher. He liked to have Nikki's chocolates available as special treats for his students. He was so popular that the man's students visited him at home in the summer. After Tori and Lidia finished their phone calls, they helped Nikki with the other customers who had appeared. Nikki went into the kitchen and started making some chocolates to order for a customer who was picking them up that day.

The customer had wanted strawberry flavored caramels. Nikki got out the brown sugar, butter, and cream and started mixing the caramels. She added some strawberry flavoring and shaped them on the tray. After she popped them into the refrigerator, she went to the front of the store. It was busy, but Tori and Lidia had it under control. Just then the door opened, and Seth appeared.

"How was the station today?" Nikki asked him. Seth was her college age son who was studying criminal justice. He was home for the summer and holding down two separate part-time jobs. He worked for Nikki in the afternoon and the police department during the morning. He was on desk duty, so he was able to observe the action without getting too involved. Nikki was happy that he'd found his calling, but she still worried about him choosing to follow in her shoes. Nikki's father had been in the FBI. Nikki had wanted to go to the academy, but she had gotten married instead. Her husband turned out to be a cheating liar and had left her and Seth high and dry in Atlanta. Nikki had decided to move to Maple Hills to get away from the big city.

"It was a good day," said Seth, grabbing a cup of coffee.

"Did your mom tell you her new idea?" Tori asked him while giving him a kiss. Tori and Seth had been dating for a few months now. Nikki approved. Tori helped keep Seth grounded, and they made a cute couple.

"What new idea?" Seth asked Nikki.

"I am thinking of serving milkshakes over the summer," she said.

"With homemade ice cream," chimed in Tori. Nikki smiled.

"That sounds wonderful," said Seth. "I remember you making ice cream when I was little. You used to get fresh peaches and make peach ice cream with them."

"Oh, that sounds delicious," said Tori.

"It was," insisted Seth. "It would be so hot outside, but the peach ice cream cooled us down."

Nikki smiled. She remembered making the ice cream. She made a mental note to see if she could find some fresh peaches or have them shipped up from Atlanta.

"Did you see the chief today?" Nikki asked Seth.

"Yes. He assigned me my own desk today," said Seth proudly. The chief was Chief Daily, head of the police department and a dear friend of Nikki's.

"I'm filling out forms and running errands," Seth said. "Don't worry, Mom. I am nowhere near the criminals," he reassured Nikki.

"I'm glad you're enjoying your job," said Nikki.

"I am enjoying it," Seth said while rinsing out his cup and moving behind the counter. "I also enjoy working here with you. I'm glad to be able to take some of the burden of running the store off your shoulders."

The door opened, and a good-looking, tall man walked in. He had on jeans and a t-shirt. He walked over to Nikki and gave her a kiss.

"Hi, Hawk," said Nikki, smiling. "How's your day going?"

"You know, lots of desk work," he said, frowning. Hawk was Nikki's boyfriend. He was also a detective and the son of Chief Daily. He had helped Seth get his part-time job on the force.

"Oh, poor baby," Nikki teased. She knew Hawk would rather be out and about than tied to a desk.

"Mom and I were just talking about milkshakes," Seth chimed in.

"Milkshakes?" Hawk asked.

"Yes," said Nikki. "I was thinking about putting in a milkshake machine and ice cream freezer. It's finally getting warm, and milkshakes help keep people cool."

Hawk agreed with Nikki. "What flavors were you thinking of making?" he asked.

"Well, there has already been a demand for peach, and I suppose I should do vanilla and chocolate," Nikki said.

"How about blueberry?" Tori asked.

"That's a great idea," said Nikki. "We should have some fresh ones coming into season soon."

"Those sound delicious," Lidia added. "We could do a special flavor each week."

"What a great idea," said Nikki. "We could have apple and pineapple."

"Or mocha," said Lidia.

"Or pumpkin," said Seth. They all looked at him. "What?" he asked.

"Summer flavors," Nikki reminded him. Everyone laughed.

"Okay, then how about blackberry? There is a pick-all-you-can farm about twenty minutes from here, and they advertised blackberries," said Seth.

"That sounds yummy," said Tori. "And don't forget strawberry," she added.

"We could make a fourth of July cone with vanilla, strawberry, and blueberry," suggested Nikki.

"Very patriotic," Hawk teased.

"Well, what is your idea? I haven't heard from you yet."

"I think you should make egg creams," he replied.

"Egg creams? What are those?" asked Nikki. She had been living in the north for a while, but no one had ever mentioned egg creams before.

"You have never had an egg cream?" asked Lidia.

"No. Do they have raw egg in them? They sound kind of gross," said Nikki.

"Oh my goodness," said Tori. "We will have to make some. It is better to taste them than to explain them."

"Okay," said Nikki.

"I'll be back in a few minutes. Lidia could you put some glasses in the freezer?" asked Tori. Lidia agreed, and Tori walked out of the store. Nikki laughed. A few minutes later, she returned. She was carrying a bag. She put the bag on the counter and pulled out some milk, chocolate syrup, and seltzer.

Nikki looked at the ingredients questioningly. "Trust me," said Tori noticing the troubled look. Nikki shrugged, and Tori went to work. By the time she was done she had five tall glasses filled with egg cream. Nikki and Seth each took a glass and tried a sip. They both smiled.

"This is incredible," said Nikki. "I'll have to feature Tori's egg creams when we open the milkshake stand."

Seth agreed. They enjoyed their cool beverages and the lull in customers. Then the door opened, and a few people walked in.

"I'll take care of them," declared Lidia.

"Thank you," said Nikki. She handed Lidia a napkin

and pointed to her upper lip. "You have an egg cream mustache." Lidia laughed while she wiped it off. She thanked Nikki and went to help the customers.

"What are your lunch plans?" Nikki asked Hawk.

"It's funny you should ask," he replied. "I was thinking of taking Seth out to lunch. I want to talk with him about work stuff."

Seth looked up with a smile. "Do you mind, Mom? I'd love to pick Hawk's brain about different cases."

"It's true," said Hawk. "He keeps me on my toes, just like his mom."

"That's fine with me," said Nikki. "We're not too busy right now. You can start when lunch is done."

Seth thanked her, and Hawk smiled. They both got up, and Hawk kissed Nikki goodbye. "I'll see you later," he said as they walked toward the door.

Nikki was delighted that Hawk was taking Seth under his wing. Seth had changed his major in college a while ago to reflect what he saw as a strength in Nikki. He told her she was the reason he was going into criminal justice. Nikki was thrilled that he was pursuing something that he liked. She wished him the best and hoped he would not get hurt. She was glad that he had the chief and Hawk to look up to. Those were the two men in town Nikki could count on to always have her back. From the start, they had been kind and loyal to her. Nikki looked out the window and watched Seth and Hawk walk to the diner. Seth was talking animatedly, and Hawk was nodding in encouragement. Nikki smiled knowing that Hawk only wanted the best for Seth and her. After dealing with a former husband who cheated, Nikki had been gun-shy when it came to relationships. She was glad to feel safe and comfortable around Hawk. She made a mental note to make him some of his favorite chocolates as a thank you. Nikki turned and looked around the store. She mentally saw the way the milkshake and float counter would fit in. *Maybe I should buy everyone those pointy hats the soda jerks used to wear,* she thought. She laughed at the image of Hawk wearing one of those hats. Nikki walked into the kitchen and started making some chocolates for Hawk. She pulled out the dark chocolate and opened the refrigerator. There were fresh strawberries. Nikki pulled them out and melted the chocolate. *Hawk will love these,* she thought as she dipped the strawberries in the chocolate.

2

Nikki heard the phone ring in the shop. She waited and heard Tori answer. Tori called out for Nikki, and Nikki put down the last strawberry she had been dipping. The strawberries looked and smelled delicious.

"I'll be right there," she told Tori. Nikki took off her apron and washed her hands. She walked into the store and picked up the phone.

"Hello?" she said. There was no answer. "Hello," she repeated. There was silence and then the phone went dead. *Probably a wrong number*, Nikki thought. She asked Tori what the caller had wanted, but Tori said the caller had merely asked for the owner. Tori said it was a male voice, but beyond that she didn't know who it was. Nikki looked at the phone and saw that the number was unknown. Nikki was put off for a moment, but then she saw the store was getting busy. She put the phone down and ran back to the kitchen to put Hawk's strawberries in the refrigerator. Nikki then went back to the front of the store and started to wait on customers. Nikki, Tori, and Lidia had been steadily busy since Valentine's Day. The mayor's daughter had gotten married that holiday and had requested a special order of Nikki's chocolates for her rehearsal dinner and reception. Nikki had to admit that her business had picked up afterwards. She was not complaining. The three women were kept busy that day for about an hour. Seth and Hawk came back from lunch smiling in a conspiratorial way. Nikki wondered what they were up to, but Hawk just smiled and waved goodbye. Nikki supposed he had to go back to his office. Seth joined her behind the counter.

"Did you have a good lunch?" she asked him.

"Yes," he said. He grabbed some chocolates from the back and started restocking the case.

"What did you guys talk about?" Nikki asked.

"You know, work stuff," said Seth. "Why don't you go and grab a bite to eat," he suggested to Nikki. "We can hold down the fort."

Nikki realized it was past her usual lunchtime. She decided to take Seth up on his offer. Nikki asked Lidia if she wanted to go to lunch with her.

"Sure," said Lidia. Seth had brought Tori a sandwich, so she could sit in the kitchen and eat while keeping an eye on the store.

"Where do you want to go?" asked Nikki.

"There is the new sandwich shop across the square. Does that sound good to you?" suggested Lidia.

"Sure," said Nikki. She was going to grab her jacket, but she opened the door first.

"What perfect weather," Nikki said, deciding to ignore her jacket. "Let's go."

After lunch, Nikki walked back to the store. It was quiet. Tori was in the back, eating, and Seth was wiping down the counters.

"Thank you," Nikki said to Seth.

"You're welcome. I thought I would clean the windows in a bit."

"Really? Usually I have to twist your arm to get you to wash windows," Nikki said with a laugh.

Seth shrugged. "I'm happy to help." He smiled, but Nikki didn't notice, nor did she notice the extra bounce in his step.

Nikki spotted the mail on the counter. She grabbed a cup of coffee and sat at a table to sort through the mail. She threw out the junk and put the bills aside to be sorted and opened later. Fortunately, she did not dread opening the bills anymore. She sat back and sipped her coffee. The door opened, and a tall woman with jet-black hair walked in. Nikki did not recognize her. She was made up and wore jeans and a dressy top. The woman walked to the counter and asked Tori what was good. While Tori was showing her the chocolates, the woman looked around the shop. She seemed to dismiss her surroundings and then she saw Nikki. When she looked at her, Nikki felt like daggers were piercing her skin. It had been a while since she felt that uncomfortable. The feeling reminded her of when her ex-husband would look at her after having too much to drink, right before he started yelling at her. Nikki shivered. The woman shifted her gaze back to Tori. Nikki stood up and walked over to the counter.

"Can I help you?" Nikki asked, a bit defensively.

"No," the woman answered dismissively. The woman paid for her order and left. Nikki walked over to the counter and asked Tori what the woman had said to her. Tori shrugged.

"She just asked who the owner was. I pointed to you."

"Did you see the way she was looking at me?" Nikki asked.

"No, I was wrapping her order. What was she doing?"

Nikki thought about telling Tori about the feeling the woman had caused, but then she stopped. *Maybe I was making something out of nothing,* she thought.

"Never mind," she told Tori. "It was probably my imagination." Nikki started to walk back toward the kitchen. The odd phone call and the woman's stare had her on edge. A child burst into the shop and ran past her, yelling. Nikki jumped and caught herself before she said something to the child. A few seconds later, his mother walked in and chastised the child for running around. Nikki decided she should stay in the quiet kitchen for a while. She went in the kitchen and asked Lidia if she would help Tori on the floor. Lidia agreed, but she noticed Nikki's mood. She walked to the front of the store and left Nikki alone in the kitchen. Nikki checked the chocolate covered strawberries and saw that they would be ready in about an hour. Nikki then sat down and sorted through her orders. She found a couple that needed to be started, and she got up and pulled out the ingredients. When she reached for the flour, it slipped out of her hand and crashed to the floor. She stooped down to pick it up and started to shake. The tears came a few seconds later. Nikki felt a gentle hand on her shoulder and she turned her head to see Lidia standing over her. She gently guided Nikki to a chair in the kitchen. Lidia cleaned up the flour while Nikki composed herself. When the flour was cleaned up, Lidia sat down next to Nikki. She took her hands in hers and asked what was going on.

"There was a weird phone call this morning, and a few minutes ago this woman walked in. She glared at me. When I asked if I could help her, she dismissed me and left the store. I would not have cared about that, but the way she looked at me…" Nikki shivered. "I thought she was going to hurt me."

"Was she involved with the chocolate competition?" Lidia asked. Nikki had entered and won a chocolate competition that past winter. She had also solved a mysterious death. She had made some new friends, but there were some people who had a sour taste in their mouths after she had won the contest.

Nikki thought for a moment. "No, I have never seen her before."

Lidia patted Nikki's hand. "Well, no one is going to hurt you. We are all here for you. We'll take care of you," she said this soothingly, and Nikki felt her muscles relaxing. It was nice not to be dismissed. Nikki felt loved, and that warmth helped her to regain her composure. She thanked Lidia, and Lidia offered to help her with her orders. Nikki thanked her again, and the two women got to work.

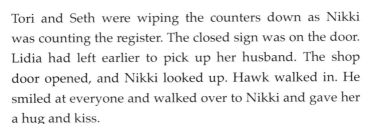

Tori and Seth were wiping the counters down as Nikki was counting the register. The closed sign was on the door. Lidia had left earlier to pick up her husband. The shop door opened, and Nikki looked up. Hawk walked in. He smiled at everyone and walked over to Nikki and gave her a hug and kiss.

"Almost done closing up?" Hawk asked.

"Yes," Nikki replied. She put the deposit in a bag.

"Would you like to go out to eat after you drop off your deposit?"

"Sure," Nikki said, smiling at him. She grabbed the deposit bag.

"I can drop that off for you," said Tori.

"Thank you," said Nikki. "If you want to come in a little later tomorrow that would be fine. Lidia and I can hold down the fort until noon."

Seth and Tori thanked her. Seth told Nikki they were going to a concert that night and that it might run late. She imagined that allowing Tori to sleep in would be well received.

"That's fine. If you need to sleep on Tori's couch, let me know," Nikki said.

"I will call or text you later," Seth promised.

Nikki thanked him and went back to the kitchen.

"What are you doing back there?" Hawk asked.

"You'll see. Just sit down, I will be back in a minute," Nikki told Hawk. She got the strawberries out of the refrigerator and put them in a box. She wrapped them up and took them into the front of the store.

"These are for you," Nikki told Hawk as she handed him the box.

Hawk looked up at her and smiled. "What is it?"

"You'll have to open it and see," said Nikki laughing. Hawk opened the box and smiled.

"My favorites," he said, pulling one out. "What did I do to deserve this?" he asked.

"It's just a thank you. I appreciate all that you have done for Seth and for me," said Nikki. "I love that you listen to Seth and are excited by what he says."

"He is a smart kid," said Hawk. "He gets that from his mother."

Nikki thanked him. Hawk stood up and held up a strawberry by her mouth.

"Bite?" he asked. Nikki laughed and took a bite.

"Are you ready for dinner now?" Nikki asked.

"Sure," said Hawk. "I'll leave the strawberries here, and we can grab them after dinner."

"Okay," said Nikki.

Hawk grabbed Nikki's jacket. She thanked him, but said she wouldn't need it that night. It was still warm outside, and Nikki was enjoying not wearing a heavy winter coat. Hawk offered to carry her jacket for her, and Nikki thanked him. They locked up the chocolate shop and started walking down the sidewalk, hand in hand. There was a gentle breeze blowing, and Nikki noticed the other people who were walking had a slight spring in their step. *Warmer weather will do that to you*, she thought. Just then, Nikki noticed a car moving slowly on her left. She turned her head and saw a dark-haired woman driving. The woman looked right at Nikki and glared.

Nikki slowed down and Hawk turned his head toward the car.

"What do you want?" Nikki asked the driver loudly. The driver did not answer. Hawk stepped toward the car. The woman turned her head forward, accelerated quickly, and drove away, screeching the tires as she left. Nikki started shaking. Hawk put his arm around her shoulder and comforted her.

"What was that about?" asked Hawk.

"I honestly don't know," said Nikki. "She showed up in the shop earlier today and glared at me the whole time."

"Did she buy anything?" asked Hawk.

"Yes. Tori waited on her. When she looked at Tori, she smiled. When she looked at me it was like I had killed her cat or something."

"That's weird," said Hawk. "Did she look familiar to you?"

"No, why? Did she look familiar to you?"

"No, I just wanted to make sure there were no hard feelings out there about the candy contest or something."

"Lidia said the same thing. I didn't recognize that woman, though. I have never seen her before today," replied Nikki. "Do you think you can look into this?" she asked Hawk.

"Sure. I will get on it first thing tomorrow morning. It looked like a local rental. I can call the shops and ask if anyone matching her description has rented any cars lately."

"Thank you," said Nikki, giving Hawk a hug and kiss. "I feel safer with you around."

"You can take care of yourself," Hawk reassured her.

"I know," Nikki said. "But, it is nice to have you by my side."

Hawk looked into Nikki's eyes. He pulled her close and kissed her again. "There is no need to worry. I have your back. Now, let's get to the diner and eat something." Hawk put his arm around Nikki's shoulder and walked with her to the diner. They opened the diner door and the owner told them to take a seat. Hawk picked a comfy booth and ordered some coffee for them. They ordered their dinner and talked while they were waiting for their food. Nikki told Hawk again how much she appreciated him taking Seth under his wing.

"It's really been a pleasure for me," Hawk told Nikki. "Seth is intelligent and eager to work. The chief loves having him around. He sorted through a box worth of old files today. The chief had wanted me to do that, but I've been too busy with my own paperwork. So, believe me, I'm glad to have Seth around."

Nikki smiled and sipped her coffee. She looked out the window at the park and was happy to see the new green leaves on the trees. Spring was in full bloom, and summer was right around the corner. The waiter came by and gave them their dinner.

"Dig in," said Hawk, reaching for his fork.

"Will do," smiled Nikki.

3

H awk and Nikki were just finishing dinner when Nikki's phone rang. It was Seth.

"Mom, you need to come by the shop. The window in the door is broken, and it looks like someone robbed the store."

"Wait, weren't you and Tori going out tonight?"

"We were. We stopped by Tori's to eat something and on our way out of town we drove by the shop. I noticed the glass was broken. I'm in the store right now. The money you keep in the register is still here. I thought I would look in the kitchen."

"Get out of there. Do not go into the kitchen," Nikki demanded. Hawk looked up. Nikki pantomimed paying the bill. "Call the police. We're on our way."

Hawk was waiting to pay the bill, and Nikki told him what had happened. The owner overheard them and told them to get out of there, dinner was on him. Nikki thanked him, and she and Hawk ran out of the shop. Hawk called his father, Chief Daily, and filled him in. Nikki and Hawk ran down the street toward the chocolate shop.

When they arrived, Seth and Tori were outside. Seth told Nikki he had called the police, and they all heard sirens coming their way. Hawk told them to wait there. He pulled out his gun and went into the shop. Nikki waited anxiously. She did not enjoy waiting. A few minutes later, he reemerged.

"It's all clear. There's no one inside," he reassured Nikki.

Nikki let out a breath she didn't realize she was holding and thanked him. She told Seth about the woman from earlier. Seth was concerned, but Nikki told him it probably wasn't related to the break-in. She just wanted him to be aware of the situation.

The police arrived and cordoned off the sidewalk in front of the shop. Nikki and Hawk took advantage of the cordon and went into the shop to look around. The counters were still intact, and the register was not opened. The trophy from the candy competition had been moved and other things on the shelves had been pushed out of the way. Hawk's chocolates were on the floor. They looked like they had been stepped on. There were boxes and papers all over the floor. Nikki dreaded going into the kitchen, but she bravely opened the door. There was flour and sugar strewn all over the tables and floors. Some canisters had been pushed aside and dumped. The refrigerators were intact, but the shelves had been messed up. Some candies were ruined, but most were left untouched. Nikki was glad she locked most of her candy in the shelves in the front. She had intended on putting them in the refrigerator after work. Thinking about it, Nikki realized most of the loose chocolates would keep in the display overnight. Nikki could feel the tears well up in her eyes, but she stubbornly wiped them away. There was too much going on for her to start crying. Hawk came up behind her and took her hand. He gave it a squeeze and gave her a hug. Nikki and Hawk went back outside. A young officer was talking to Seth, and Seth turned when Nikki came out of the shop.

"Are forensics here yet?" Hawk asked the officer.

"Not yet, Detective Daily, but they should be here any minute," the officer responded.

"Okay. I want them to dust for prints," Hawk said.

"I will let them know," said the officer.

The forensic team pulled up, and the officer walked over to them. An older, graying woman got out of the car and the officer proceeded to fill her in. The woman was wearing a suit and carried a black bag. She carried herself as if she were in charge. The woman looked over and saw Hawk. She walked over to where Hawk and Nikki were standing.

"Good evening, Hawk," she said and held out her hand.

"Hi, Leah," he replied, shaking her hand. Leah said hello to Nikki. Leah was the head of the forensics department. She had worked for the department longer than Hawk, and she knew what she was doing. Hawk learned everything he knew about forensics from watching her and listening to what she told him. Nikki knew this because Hawk would go on and on at dinner some nights discussing the different aspects of his cases. Her name came up quite a bit.

"I heard the address over the radio and thought I should come on by and make sure everyone was okay. Also, your dad called me to make sure I was on my way." She laughed at Hawk.

"Thank you for coming, Leah. I already went in. We were careful where we walked, and we didn't touch anything. It looks like a break-in but not a robbery," Hawk said. "Either way, I would like it dusted for prints."

"That's fine, but I have to tell you, you might not get any leads in a case like this," Leah replied. "There are so many people coming in and out of the store, it could be hard to figure out just who broke in."

"I understand," said Hawk, "but if anyone can do it, you can." He smiled at Leah, and she laughed.

"Okay," Leah said. "My guys are in there dusting right now." She turned to Nikki, "Could you give me a list of employees who worked today and customers who came in?"

"Seth, Tori, and Lidia were all in today. I can look at the receipts and give you a list of customers. There was one, though, that I did not know."

Leah looked at Nikki with a raised eyebrow. "Really?" she asked.

"Yes. All of the other customers were from town, but she was not. I didn't recognize her, and she paid with cash."

"She may have been scoping the place out," Leah suggested. "Was there anything else of value in the shop?"

"Not really," said Nikki. "It seems like whoever did

this was looking for something. They didn't mess with the cash register. I don't know what they were looking for. Nothing is missing. It is all just a big mess," she told Leah.

"Okay. Let my guys do their magic, and you get me that list as soon as possible, please."

"I will," Nikki assured her. Leah went over to the shop to see how her forensic team was progressing. As she walked in, Hawk and Nikki could hear her barking out orders. Hawk turned to Nikki.

"I'm glad Leah is on the case. Do we have everyone's fingerprints down at the station?" he asked Nikki.

"Yes, you do," said Nikki. There had been a few other incidents since Nikki had moved to Maple Hills, and all of her employees had been fingerprinted at one time or another.

"Who would do this?" Nikki asked. Hawk put his arm around her comfortingly. She could feel her eyes watering up. "I'll make you some more chocolates tomorrow."

"Don't even worry about the chocolates. I appreciate them, and they were delicious. I love you and thank you. I don't know who would do this to you or why. I'll look into that woman with the dark hair tonight," Hawk reassured Nikki. "If she rented that car anywhere near here I will know about it by tomorrow morning. I have most of the rental store owners' home phone numbers. It's one of the benefits of living in a small town. I think my dad goes fishing with one of them. When I go to the office, I'll see if he's willing to reach out to him."

"Thank you. It is just disconcerting not knowing who she is," Nikki said.

"Do you want me to stop by the house later tonight?" asked Hawk.

Before Nikki could answer, Leah was there. She apologized for interrupting.

"Well, we got what we need," she said. "I will start processing this tonight. Chief has already announced we will be working overtime on this."

"Thank you, Leah," Nikki said.

"I just hope we catch whoever did this to you," Leah answered. She shook hands with Hawk and Nikki, and she turned and walked to her car. She drove off toward the station, the forensic team following in her wake.

"I need to call Lidia," Nikki said. "I don't want her hearing about this from someone else, or walking in tomorrow morning and finding the store looking like this." She called Lidia and explained what happened. Lidia offered to come over and help clean up, but Nikki told her to stay home. She said she had enough help with Seth there.

"So, can I start cleaning up now?" Nikki asked Hawk.

"I suppose so, but don't you want to go home and get some rest?" he asked Nikki.

"I thought about that," she replied, "but I don't want to give whoever did this any satisfaction. Also, I'm not sure I would be able to sleep after this. I can open tomorrow, right?"

"Yes, you can," Hawk said.

"Okay then. I am going to stay and get the shop in order. Seth, could you help me clean up?"

"Sure, Mom," Seth replied. He walked over to Tori and

spoke to her. She nodded, hugged him, and got into her car.

"What did you say to Tori?" Nikki asked.

"I told her I needed to stay with you tonight. She understands. I told her to find a friend to take to the concert. There was no reason we should both miss it."

"Are you sure?" Nikki asked. "I can get this cleaned up by myself."

"I know you could, but I want to be with you, Mom. I am willing to help, and I do not want you to be alone tonight," Seth insisted. Nikki thanked him and told Hawk what was going on. Hawk smiled at Seth and thanked him.

"I'm going to the station then," Hawk told Nikki. "If you need anything, just give me a call."

"Thank you, Hawk. We should be fine here."

They hugged, and Hawk took his car to the station. Nikki turned to Seth.

"Okay, first we get a garbage bag and cover the door. I don't want anyone getting cut on the sharp edges," Nikki said.

Seth agreed, and he walked into the shop and got the bag. Seth held the bag to the door, and Nikki duct taped it. After they finished with the door, Nikki got two brooms and some cloths. They started wiping the counters and picking up the things that had been moved. Nikki picked up the candy she had made for Hawk. *At least he got to taste it*, she thought. An hour later, they were still cleaning.

After what seemed like forever, the front of the store was almost done.

"I think I can start in the back now," Nikki told Seth. "I am going to grab a mop and bucket. Would you mind mopping this floor while I start cleaning off the tables in the kitchen? It will be better to clean the flour and sugar with something dry before we mop in there."

"Okay," Seth replied. "After I sweep in here, I'll mop and then be right with you."

Just then the phone rang. Nikki wondered who would be calling so late. She moved to answer the phone and suddenly Seth bounded over saying, "Maybe it's Tori." He picked up the phone. He listened for a second, and he seemed to turn a bit pale. He sat down hard on a nearby chair. "Dad?" he asked.

4

Nikki practically jumped over the counter to get to the phone. She grabbed it out of Seth's hand. Seth looked at her in wonderment.

"Who is this? Why are you calling here?" she demanded.

"Nikki, it's me, Andrew," the voice on the other end said. Nikki turned pale. She would know that drawl anywhere. It was her ex-husband. He had abandoned her in Atlanta to move to California with a woman Nikki had never met. After all that time, Nikki had never heard from him. Andrew had not contacted Nikki until now.

"I have nothing to say to you," Nikki said, starting to hang up the phone.

"Nikki, *listen* to me," Andrew pleaded. "I have something to tell you. It's important. It could impact you and Seth."

Nikki hesitated. She thought about just slamming the phone down, but then she reconsidered. If what he had to say impacted Seth, she needed to hear Andrew out. She put the phone back up to her ear.

"What have you done?" she asked.

"It's not like that," Andrew said. "I'm in town and want to meet with you."

"Why?" asked Nikki. "What could be so important? We haven't talked since you left, and now suddenly you call out of the blue and want to meet?"

"Can we meet tomorrow?" Andrew asked, evading Nikki's questions. Nikki didn't want to meet with Andrew. Not tomorrow, not ever. However, he said this could concern Seth. She had to meet with Andrew to find out what was going on. She thought for a moment and then replied.

"Okay, but I'm not coming alone. We'll meet in a public place. You are not to see or talk to Seth," Nikki replied.

"That's fine," Andrew said.

"We are not going to meet in my shop. That is *my* shop. It has not been stained by your presence. There's a park in the middle of town. There's a bench there near a table. I will meet you there at noon tomorrow. Then I don't want to ever see you again," Nikki said.

"Okay, we will meet then," Andrew agreed, "at the bench by the table. Thank you, Nikki."

Nikki hung up the phone and fell into a chair beside Seth.

"What is going on, Mom?" Seth asked. "Was that really Dad?"

"I'm not sure what's happening, and yes, that was your father," Nikki replied. "I'm meeting him in the park tomorrow at noon."

"I want to go with you," said Seth. "I don't trust him."

"Absolutely not," retorted Nikki. "He does not deserve to see or speak to you. I need to meet with him and find out what he wants."

"Okay, but I don't want you going alone," said Seth.

"I won't," said Nikki, picking up her cell phone. She placed a call.

"Hawk?" she asked. "I need to talk to you. Andrew called. He wants to meet with me." Hawk merely told her to stay at the shop, and they hung up. About a minute went by, and a car screeched to a halt outside the shop. Hawk flew in and picked Nikki up in his arms. He held her close and whispered in her ear. Nikki put her head on his chest and started crying. Hawk just held on to her. He comforted her and after a few minutes Nikki stopped crying. Hawk handed her his handkerchief. She wiped her eyes and blew her nose.

"You know I'm going to that meeting with you," Hawk stated. It was not a question. Nikki's eyes glistened.

"Thank you," she whispered and hugged him hard. Hawk held on to Nikki for a little while longer. When he knew she had stopped crying, he relaxed his hold. Nikki sniffed and wiped her eyes.

"What does he want?" asked Hawk.

"I don't know," Nikki said. "He evaded my questions and wouldn't tell me why he was here or what he wanted." She was frustrated and scared, but she was glad that Hawk was there.

"Well, we'll find out together then, won't we?" reassured Hawk. "You're safe with me."

"Thank you," said Nikki. It was nice to have Hawk in

her corner. She felt a little better about meeting Andrew at the park the next day.

"Okay," said Hawk. "Now, what do I need to do here to help get this store ready to open tomorrow?"

Nikki looked at him. "What about the mystery woman?" she asked.

"She can wait until the morning. I have a real woman I need to take care of right now," Hawk said, smiling. Seth put a pot of coffee on, and they continued to clean up the store. Hawk and Nikki took the shelves, and Seth cleaned up the flour and sugar.

"I could have made so much candy with that flour and sugar," Nikki mused.

"I'll go to the store early tomorrow morning and pick some up for you," offered Seth.

"Thank you," said Nikki. She was glad she could rely on Seth.

When they put the last canister back on the shelf, Hawk got a call. He walked into the front of the store. Nikki could hear him talking. She followed behind him.

"Hello? Yes? Thank you, I'll tell her," Hawk hung up and looked at Nikki.

"That was Leah," he told Nikki after putting his cell phone on the table. "She said there are no breaks in the case, but they'll continue working on it tomorrow."

"I am glad they are so committed to helping us."

"That is their job," said Hawk.

"Yes, but Leah and the forensic team are going above and beyond basic work," said Nikki.

"She just wants you to be safe," Hawk told Nikki.

"I appreciate that," Nikki said. Seth told her he was

done sweeping the kitchen. Nikki thanked him and told him it was time to go home.

"We need to sleep as much as we can. It'll be a busy day tomorrow," she said.

Seth agreed. He turned out the lights, and Nikki and Hawk followed him outside. There was a police officer standing there. Nikki looked at Hawk for answers.

"That is just a precaution. You can't lock your shop, so Richard here will be watching it until he is relieved in a few hours."

"Thank you, Richard," Nikki said.

"It's my pleasure," Richard replied.

"Can I get you a cup of coffee?" Nikki asked.

"No, thank you. I filled up before I came on duty," Richard replied.

"Okay, but the next time you're in the shop, the coffee is on me," insisted Nikki.

Nikki and Seth started to walk to her car.

"Would you like me to follow you home?" asked Hawk.

This time Nikki did not refuse. Hawk followed them, and Nikki made up her sofa. Hawk told her he was going to read a bit and then go to sleep. Nikki made her way up the stairs and to her bed. She was not sure she would be able to sleep, but she was glad that Hawk was there to watch over her and Seth.

The next morning, Nikki made breakfast for Seth and Hawk. Hawk was usually the first one up, but Nikki had trouble sleeping the night before. She kept waking up with visions of Andrew in her head. Finally, Nikki decided to make breakfast. She went downstairs and crept by Hawk sleeping on the sofa. She walked quietly into the kitchen in her sweats and socks. She looked out the window and saw the sun starting to rise. It was quiet in the house, and the birds were just waking up outside. A tired squirrel scampered across her lawn and found a nut to bury. Nikki smiled at the scenery. She started some coffee and pulled the eggs and bacon out of the fridge. She mixed the eggs with some milk, salt, and pepper, and pulled out the frying pan. Nikki put the bacon in the frying pan and cooked it. By this time, she thought she heard Hawk stirring in the front room. She poured two cups of coffee and finished cooking the bacon.

"Good morning," she heard Hawk say as he walked into the kitchen. His hair was rumpled, and he had slept in his clothes from the night before. Hawk had stashed some of his clothes at Nikki's house, though, so at least he would look presentable at work this morning.

"Good morning," she replied, turning around and giving him a quick kiss.

"Let me take over breakfast," he suggested.

"Okay," Nikki said. She was too tired to put up an argument. Nikki sat at the table and watched Hawk finish the bacon and start the eggs.

"You did not sleep well," Hawk said.

"How could you tell?" she asked.

"You got up before me. That never happens unless you're stressed about something."

"Very observant," she quipped.

"That's what I get paid for." Hawk smiled and turned off the stove. "The eggs are ready."

"Did you say the eggs are ready?" asked Seth as he walked into the kitchen wiping his eyes. He had on shorts and a t-shirt.

"Yes. Pull up a chair, and I'll get you a plate," said Hawk. Seth thanked him and poured a cup of coffee. He refilled Hawk and Nikki's cups. They all sat down and ate quietly thinking about the day ahead.

"So, I figured I would go into work this morning and meet you at the shop around 11:30. Will that work for you?" Hawk asked Nikki.

"Sounds good," she replied. She was nervous, but she didn't want to show it in front of Seth.

"I'll pick up those groceries," said Seth.

"Why don't you go back to bed," suggested Nikki. "Lidia and I can open the shop. One of us can run out for flour and sugar. Tori can swing by and pick you up on her way in."

"I know you can handle yourself, but I'm concerned that it will just be you and Lidia there," said Seth. Nikki knew he was concerned about Andrew. She didn't know what to expect, so how could Seth?

"Actually, she'll have an officer outside the shop," said Hawk.

"Okay," said Seth, Hawk's comment seemed to calm him. He got up and hugged Nikki. "Thank you, Mom. I really am tired…and I didn't even go to the concert…" He went back upstairs, and Nikki cleared up the breakfast dishes.

"Let me help you with those," said Hawk. Nikki

thanked him. Hawk washed, and Nikki dried and put them away. They got them done in no time.

"I'll get dressed, and we can go," said Nikki.

"Okay. I'll get changed, and I'll call the station to see if they've got any leads yet."

Nikki got dressed and went back downstairs. Hawk told her there were no new leads, but he would be working on finding the mystery woman that morning. Nikki thanked Hawk, and he drove her into work.

Nikki got in and found Lidia in the front of the shop getting ready to open the store. Nikki had called her the previous night to fill her in on what had happened. When Lidia saw Nikki, she walked over and gave her a hug.

"Good morning," Lidia said. "Do they know who did this?"

"Good morning," Nikki replied. "Not yet. The police are still working on it."

"Okay," said Lidia. "I figured you would want to open despite what happened. People will want chocolate either way."

You know me so well, Nikki thought. "Absolutely," she said, putting on an apron.

"We will need to get some more flour and sugar this morning."

"I'll be happy to pick it up in a bit," said Lidia. "I guess this does put a damper on the whole milkshake fountain idea."

"No," said Nikki determinedly. "I'm going to make that happen." Lidia smiled at her, and Nikki smiled back.

The front door opened, and a man walked in. Nikki flinched, but it was not Andrew. *Will I be like this all day*, she thought. The man walked over to Nikki and introduced himself.

"Hawk sent me over to hang around inside the shop. I'm an undercover detective. Would that be convenient for you?" he asked, showing Nikki his badge.

"That will be fine," said Nikki. "Why don't you sit in this corner table? It offers a good view of the shop and the front door."

"Okay. Are there any back doors?" he asked.

"Yes, but it's kept locked and dead-bolted during the day."

"Okay. I'll sit here and stay out of your way," the detective said. Nikki smiled. She felt quite reassured by the presence of the detective, and she was glad Hawk had thought to send him. She grabbed the detective some coffee and a muffin. He thanked her.

The door opened, and a familiar customer walked in. The detective sat up, but Nikki told him she knew this customer. It was the mother of the young boy who had run through the shop the other day.

"Hi, I wanted to apologize for my child's behavior the other day," she said to Nikki.

"It's no problem. I have a son, although he's a lot older now, and I know how wound up they can be at that age. Add sugar to the mix, and they'll be running for hours."

"Thank you for understanding," the woman said. "I

would like to get a pound of chocolate for my mother. It's her birthday today. Do you gift wrap?"

"Yes, we do," said Lidia coming over from behind the counter. "Let me show you what we have today." Lidia led the woman to the counter, and Nikki went into the kitchen. There were a few special orders to be made, but Tori could handle them when she and Seth came in. Nikki sat down and put her head in her hands. *I'll just shut my eyes for a bit,* she thought. A few minutes later, she heard Lidia calling her. She got up and went into the front of the store. Hawk was there.

"Why are you here so early?"

"Early?" asked Hawk. "It's 11:30."

"What?" asked Nikki. She was shocked. She looked at Lidia.

"You fell asleep. I didn't have the heart to wake you up. Tori and Seth are here early, and we handled the customers. I picked up the sugar and flour after they got here."

"Thank you, Lidia," said Nikki. "I guess the stress has gotten to me."

"Seth filled us in about Andrew. I will keep an eye on Seth and Tori when you go to meet him," Lidia promised.

"And, my detective will be here the whole time," reassured Hawk.

"Thank you, both," replied Nikki getting two mugs of coffee. "Would you like to sit down while we wait?" she asked Hawk.

"Sure," he replied, pulling out a chair for Nikki. They sat down together and Hawk filled her in on his morning.

"We canvassed the neighborhood, and no other buildings were broken into. We believe this was targeted at you."

Nikki shivered and then stopped. She did not want Hawk to worry about her. He had too much else on his mind. And, she was perfectly capable of taking care of herself. She had been doing it for many years. Still, Nikki was worried. She could not figure out who would want to break into her shop. There were some suspects but no motives or evidence. *That woman could have been scoping the shop,* she thought. *What if Andrew had done this?* She sighed. The door opened, and another customer walked in. She waved to Nikki. Nikki waved back. Seth greeted her and helped her at the counter. Nikki looked at the clock. It was almost noon.

"Well, are you ready to do this?" Hawk asked.

Nikki nodded, but she doubted herself. *Nope,* she thought. "Sure," she told Hawk out loud. Hawk helped her out of her chair and took her hand. They walked toward the door.

"Mom, are you sure you don't want me there?" Seth asked.

"Yes. Whatever he wants, I don't want you to be involved. I've known him long enough. This might be something small, but it could also be something that could rock our world."

Seth nodded. She knew he understood. Andrew had made their lives miserable. Nikki was not too excited to see him again. However, she had Hawk with her, and that almost made everything okay. Nikki squeezed Hawk's hand, and they walked out of the chocolate shop.

5

Nikki and Hawk walked out into the sunshine and cool breeze. Nikki looked across at the park and squinted to try to see the bench. She knew the bench was too far away for her to see, but she wanted to try anyway. There were a few people in the park but not too many. Some mothers were gathered with their children having a picnic. A couple walked along the trail holding hands. A father threw a football with his son. *That's something Seth missed out on thanks to Andrew,* Nikki thought. Hawk took Nikki's hand as they walked across the street. Nikki scanned people's faces as they walked, bracing herself for her first glimpse of Andrew. People she knew said hello to her. Hawk said hello to someone he worked with. Nikki kept looking around. They crossed the park and looked toward the bench. There was no one there. Nikki breathed a sigh of relief. *Maybe he's not coming,* she hoped. Then she looked at a nearby table. There was a man sitting on the table looking at his cell phone. He had dark wavy hair. The man looked up, and his blue eyes pierced Nikki's heart. She gasped. Hawk looked at her and then glanced over at the table.

"Is that him?" he asked.

"Yes," said Nikki. Her mind was suddenly flooded with memories. She remembered her first date with Andrew. They had gone to the movies and ended up making out in the parking lot afterwards. Her mind raced forward, and she remembered when Seth was born. Andrew had rushed her in Atlanta traffic to the hospital. He got her there just in time for Seth to be born. The look on his face when he first held Seth was priceless. Nikki felt tears coming to her eyes. Then she remembered the last time she saw him. He had waved goodbye and vanished into the night. He had told her he was going out for drinks with the guys, and she never saw him again until now. She had raised Seth to be the man he was despite Andrew leaving them. Nikki had struggled and had finally made something of herself in Maple Hills. She had a house and her son was in college. She had a wonderful man in her life. It angered her that Andrew would show up here in this place she now called home. She could feel her anger mounting as she approached the table. Hawk held her hand and gave it a squeeze. The small gesture was enough to help Nikki calm down a bit.

Andrew stood up. His hair was still dark and wavy like she remembered, and he was dressed in a suit. He had a gold chain around his neck and some rings on his fingers. Nikki recognized his high school ring. She noticed there was no wedding band.

"Hello, Nikki. It's been a long time," he said as he

started to move towards her. Nikki stopped, and Hawk moved a bit in front of her. He did not block her entirely, but he made it known that Andrew was not going to get close to her. Hawk held out his hand to Andrew.

"I'm Hawk. You must be Andrew," he said, halting Andrew in his tracks. Andrew was not as tall as Hawk, and Nikki found it amusing that Andrew had to look up at Hawk when he was talking to him. She smiled.

"I am Andrew," he replied, obviously uncomfortable around Hawk. Andrew reluctantly shook Hawk's hand.

"Nikki invited me to be here today," said Hawk. "I hope there won't be any trouble."

"*I* won't start any trouble," Andrew said, backing up.

"Good," said Hawk. "Now, what did you want?"

"Well, I would like to talk to Nikki if you don't mind," said Andrew, trying to sidestep Hawk and reach Nikki.

Hawk put his hand on Andrew's chest, stopping him again. "I do mind," Hawk said. Andrew started to protest.

"Watch the suit," Andrew said.

"It's okay, Hawk. Let him go," Nikki said.

Hawk dropped his hand and stepped back but not too far. Andrew straightened out his jacket. He walked up to Nikki. He held out his hand.

"Please do not touch me," she said.

Andrew held up his hands and stepped back. "Okay."

"Now, what do you want?" asked Nikki.

"What, no hey, how's it going? Or what have you been up to?" Nikki glared at Andrew. He continued. "Okay, okay. I was wondering if anything strange had been happening to you lately. Specifically, has a tall woman with dark hair talked to you?"

Nikki was taken aback. "Wait. You don't see me for all these years, and the first thing you ask is if anything weird has happened to me? Something did happen, but to lead with that? And, no, I don't care where you've been or what you've been doing," she replied. She did not want to go into any detail about yesterday. Whatever Andrew wanted he could tell her, but she would not help him along with this uncomfortable meeting. She looked in his eyes; he seemed to be genuinely concerned, but then it had been a while. *Who knows what he is thinking now*, she thought.

"Why is this any of your business? What does it matter if a tall, dark-haired woman talked to Nikki?" Hawk asked Andrew, stepping forward again.

"Why is it yours?" Andrew sneered.

Hawk took another step forward.

"Stop it," Nikki said to Andrew. She remembered this side of him and hated it. "We were done the minute you left my house that night. What I am doing now and who I am doing it with is none of your business. I asked Hawk to be here. You just need to deal with that." Andrew arched his brow but stepped back.

Andrew cleared his throat and said, "The reason I'm asking about strange things is because of a woman I recently broke up with."

"Of course, it has to do with another woman. Did you walk out on her, too?" Nikki jeered.

Andrew flinched, "I deserve that."

Nikki was going to say he deserved even more, but she decided to hear him out.

"We were in a bad relationship," Andrew continued. "I had to leave her. She was becoming obsessed with me. She was constantly asking where I was and who I was with. I had to leave her. She was smothering me. Also, she blames *you* for our breakup." Andrew had been avoiding Nikki's gaze until he looked right at Nikki at the end of his sentence. He stared at her as if he wanted to apologize but could not say the words.

Nikki was stunned. "Is that some kind of a joke?"

"Well, I might have twisted some things around when I told her about you. I wanted to be with Karissa, and I thought I should let her know about my past relationships, especially since we have a son together." Andrew was staring at the ground again.

"Is Karissa the name of your other ex-girlfriend? Why would she blame me for anything concerning you?" Nikki asked.

Andrew looked up. "Yes, Karissa is the name of the woman I was talking about. I fell for her hard when I met her. She was going to be the one. I knew I loved her, so I had to tell her about you. We have a son together. Karissa deserved to know about my past. I may have told her that you were abusive toward me. She blames you for scarring me and making it impossible for me to commit to any other woman."

Nikki felt her blood pressure rising. "Did I hear you correctly? She thinks I scarred you? Does she know you walked out on us? Does she know why? I don't even know why. I sure as hell didn't do anything abusive towards you." Nikki was shouting by this time. She was right in Andrew's face. Hawk was standing back, letting Nikki go.

"Well, I wanted to be with her, and I didn't want her to know how awful I was to you," Andrew said.

"You *were* awful to me. You would be out with your buddies until all hours drinking. I would smell the beer on you the next morning. I never did anything to hurt you. I loved you up until the day you left. Looking back, I was wrong. I should have left you before you walked out on me. Do you know what you put Seth and me through? I had to sell the house. I had to raise our son. I had to do everything. *You* left. *You* hurt me. To tell someone else I hurt you is a flat out lie. To say that *I* hurt *you*..."

Nikki's arm moved, and she felt Hawk grab her. "He's not worth it," Hawk murmured into her ear. Nikki realized Hawk was right. She put down her arm and unclenched her fist. Nikki was glad there weren't too many people in the park.

"You need to leave now," Hawk told Andrew.

"But I need to talk to Nikki some more," Andrew protested.

"You're done talking to her," Hawk said.

Andrew reached into his pocket and handed Nikki a folded-up piece of paper. "This is my number, please call me," he said, leaning towards Nikki.

He was close enough that Nikki could smell his aftershave. She looked right at him and spit in his face. He flinched and backed away.

Andrew wiped the spit off his mouth, turned, and walked away. Nikki felt herself burning with hatred. She wanted to scream. Hawk moved toward her and put his hands on her shoulders. He turned her around and hugged her. Nikki felt safe in his embrace. She sighed and looked up.

"You should have let me slap him," she said. Hawk laughed, and they started back to the chocolate shop.

Hawk asked Nikki for the slip of paper. He entered the number into his cell phone. When Nikki asked why, he said he was going to run it when he got back to his desk.

"I want to know how true his story is," said Hawk. "Do you think he actually told Karissa that lie about you? Maybe he said that just to rile you up."

"I think he is telling the truth. That would explain her glare. And, it would give her a reason to tear up my shop. He knows that just being here is going to get me riled; he does not need to make anything up to accomplish that."

"That makes sense," said Hawk. Hawk told Nikki to put the number in her phone in case Andrew tried to call her.

"I don't want to talk to him," said Nikki.

"You don't have to. Just let me know if he bothers you or Seth anymore."

Nikki thanked him and put the number in her phone. She asked Hawk if he wanted to grab some lunch. He said yes as they walked toward the street. The park was filling up with people out for picnic lunches. Nikki loved living in a small town where people felt safe letting their children run around in a park.

"Are you sure you'll be able to eat?" Hawk asked.

"No, but I could sure use the company," Nikki said. "Maybe we should go back to the shop first and let Seth know what happened. I want to fill him in on what Andrew said. I would also like to let the officer who is stationed outside know what Andrew looks like so he can stop Andrew from coming in the shop to bother Seth while we're at lunch."

"Okay," said Hawk. "I'm sure your guard will keep Andrew away from you. They love you at the department. Maybe it's the candy you send in with Seth," Hawk joked. Nikki smiled. They turned around and started walking towards the shop.

6

Nikki and Hawk walked towards the street. Suddenly they heard a scream. It was loud and close. Nikki broke out in a run, and Hawk was right behind her. The scream had come from the area of the chocolate shop. Nikki ran over and saw the detective Hawk had assigned to the shop standing by the alley next to the shop. He was on his phone when Nikki and Hawk arrived.

"What is going on?" Hawk asked.

"What was that noise?" Nikki asked.

"There's a body in the alley," said the detective. "I've just notified the chief. He said no one is to go down the alley. The officer you had by the door is still there."

The alley was located between Nikki's chocolate store and the business next door. It was generally well kept. Nikki used one end of the alley for her garbage bins. The other end, further from the street, led to a back parking lot. The alley was well lit by the sun, which allowed Nikki and

Hawk to see the body from where they were standing. Nikki and Hawk looked at each other and nodded.

"We're going in," said Hawk.

"But the chief..." started the detective.

Hawk and Nikki pushed past the detective and walked quickly to the body in the alley. There were garbage bins around the halfway point and the body was in front of them. There was a bag of trash nearby. Even from a distance, Nikki could tell the person had dark hair. Hawk got to the body first and put on gloves. He lifted the head and nodded to Nikki. She came over, looked, and turned away.

"It's Karissa," she said to Hawk as she started walking back up the alley towards her shop. Nikki felt fear rising up in her. Even though she had seen her fair share of bodies, it never got easier, especially when she knew the person who had died. Nikki was running through the conversation she had had with Andrew in the park. Andrew had certainly been wound up when he left. Hawk caught up with her. He looked at her and she nodded. She knew Hawk was thinking the same thing. *Was Andrew capable of this*? *Had Karissa pushed him to the edge*? Nikki was scared. Hawk ran towards the park. Nikki waited by the alley opening, and Hawk reappeared a few minutes later.

"There's no sign of him," he said to Nikki. "I tried to call the number that he gave you, but there was no answer. Please go into the shop and stay there. I will put out an APB on him." Nikki watched as Hawk took out his phone and called the station. He put an APB out on Andrew. Nikki thanked him and went into the shop.

Once inside, Nikki saw Lidia, Tori, and Seth sitting at a

table. Tori was encouraging Lidia to sip on a glass of water. Lidia did not look well. Seth saw Nikki and hurried over to her. He hugged her and led her to the table. Hawk walked in and sat down next to Nikki. Blue flashing lights appeared a few minutes later, and the detective walked in. He sat down at the table and let Hawk and Nikki know what was going on.

"Your employee, Lidia, walked down the alley to take out the trash," said the detective to Nikki. "I heard her scream, and I ran outside. The guard by the door had started running down the street. I told him to get back to the door and that I would handle the situation. He ran back to the door as I ran to the alley. Your employee was in the alley next to the body. I called the police and led her back inside." He turned to Hawk. "I waited by the alley for the police to come. That's when you and Nikki showed up. I think it was a gunshot. I'm not sure." The detective looked a little green. Hawk thanked him and told him to get some water. He and Nikki went back outside. They walked back down the alley while the first police arrivals cordoned off the area.

Walking down the alley, Hawk noticed there was no sign of a struggle.

"Nothing is knocked over, and there are no scrapes or bruises on her body," he told Nikki. Nikki looked around. He was right. The only thing amiss was the garbage bag that Lidia had dropped when she saw Karissa's body.

"She must have known her killer," Hawk said. Nikki agreed. Hawk continued, "I put out an APB on Andrew. He had time to kill her after he left us in the park. Who else would she have known in Maple Hills?"

"Nobody that I know of," said Nikki. "But, as much as I hate him, I don't think Andrew is capable of killing someone."

"I know you were close, but that was a while ago," said Hawk. "People change. You don't know what he has been through since he left you."

"That's true, but I still don't think he would do this," said Nikki.

"Okay. I see what you're saying," said Hawk. "I still need to question him. Would you mind trying to call him? I really need to know where he is. He didn't answer when I called. Maybe if it's a different number, he'll pick up."

Nikki agreed to call. She dialed the number, but there was no answer. She left a message.

"Andrew, when you get this, please call me. Something has happened, and I need to speak to you. Please call me; it's urgent. It concerns Karissa." She hung up her cell phone. She and Hawk continued looking around.

"What is that over there?" asked Nikki, pointing to the wall across from Karissa's body.

"It looks like a handprint," responded Hawk. "Good eye." He took a picture, and just then the forensic team appeared. Hawk showed them the handprint and the body. Leah was there again, and she thanked Hawk for showing her team around. Hawk took Nikki's arm and led her back to the shop. As they got to the door, they heard a siren. It was an ambulance arriving to take Karissa's body to the morgue. Nikki walked into the shop. As she shut the door, she turned the closed sign to face the window.

"Hey, everyone," she said, addressing Tori, Seth, and Lidia. They all looked at her. "We will be closed the rest of today and tomorrow. I hope to reopen after that. I will call you and let you know what's going on."

Seth approached her and gave her a hug. "I think I'll take Tori home," he said.

"That's a good idea," said Nikki.

"I called Lidia's husband. He should be here any minute," said Tori.

"Thank you," said Nikki. She and the others closed down the shop. Someone was supposed to be there later that day to take care of the broken window.

"I'll keep the uniform officer on the door," Hawk offered. "He can help with the window."

"Thank you," said Nikki. Nikki thought for a moment and looked something up on her phone. She made a call.

"Yes, tomorrow would work. Thank you," she said and hung up.

"Who was that?" asked Hawk.

"I called a cleaning crew specializing in crime scenes. Do you think your teams will be done with the scene by tomorrow afternoon?"

"Yes, they should be done by then. Are you having the cleaners stop by then?"

"Yes," said Nikki.

"That sounds reasonable," said Hawk.

"We should go to the morgue and see what they have to say about Karissa," said Nikki. Hawk agreed and led her to his car. They drove to the station and walked into the morgue. They saw the chief with the medical examiner and walked in the room. Nikki checked her phone and saw that there were no missed calls. Andrew had not called her back.

.

7

In the morgue, the medical examiner and the chief were looking over Karissa's body. The medical examiner told Nikki and Hawk that Karissa had been shot around noon.

"Why didn't we hear the shot?" asked Nikki.

"The person who killed her probably had a silencer on his gun," the chief explained.

"That would make sense," said Hawk.

"Yeah, we heard Lidia scream, but we didn't know why," said Nikki.

"I noticed she was shot in the head," said Hawk to the medical examiner.

"Yes, and she was kneeling when she was shot. There were some abrasions on her knees, and she was lying backwards in the alley with her legs bent. That's how we know she was kneeling."

"Why would someone tell a person to kneel before shooting them?"

"Maybe if the person was shorter than the victim.

Having the victim kneel would give the shooter a feeling of dominance and control over the victim," Hawk said. "That being said, was Karissa taller than Andrew in her heels?" he asked Nikki.

Nikki thought about it. "Yes, she would have been a little taller than him."

"Has anyone seen Andrew yet?" Hawk asked the chief.

"No, there have been no reported sightings," the chief answered.

Nikki looked at the body on the table. She thought about Andrew. "I really do not think he did this," she told Hawk. "Yes, he's a jerk, but that doesn't make him a murderer. I know him better than anyone else in this room." She could hear her voice getting higher and feel her body tense up.

"Well, right now he is the only one with a motive. If you find someone else, I'll talk to them," snapped Hawk. Nikki held her breath. Hawk apologized.

"It's been a rough day for everyone," said the chief. "Nikki, can I speak with you privately for a minute?"

"Sure, Chief," Nikki replied. She followed him down the hall, relieved to be away from the friction in the morgue.

"Why don't you sit down? Can I get you a drink? Would you like some water? Coffee?" the chief asked.

"I'd like some coffee please, thank you," replied Nikki as she sat in a chair across from the chief's desk. There was a box of tissues on his desk. Nikki took one and wiped her eyes. The chief poured her a cup of coffee and sat down at his desk. Nikki thanked him for the coffee and took a sip.

"Nikki, you have been a great asset to this police force

ever since you came to Maple Hills. You have helped us solve quite a few cases and have been a blessing to my son. That being said, I have to wonder if you might be too close to this one. The victim was threatening you and our main suspect is your ex-husband. I would understand if you needed to back away from this one."

Nikki was not too surprised. She did let her emotions get away from her a bit in the morgue. She had never blindly questioned Hawk's suspicions about a suspect before. She thought for a moment.

"I understand why you may think I'm too close to this," she said to the chief. "However, I can be objective. I'm glad you called me out of the morgue. I just had to step back for a moment. Yes, I will be able to work this case with Hawk. If I feel my objectivity sliding, I will excuse myself. I do believe I can work this case, though."

"Okay, Nikki. I will keep you on the case for now. If I feel you're not seeing things in an objective way, though, I will pull you off the case."

"I understand. Thank you, Chief."

"Okay, now let's get back to the morgue and see what Hawk and the medical examiner have come up with."

Nikki was glad to still be on the case. She walked down the hall with the chief. When they got to the morgue, she walked over to Hawk and squeezed his hand. He looked down and smiled at her. The medical examiner continued with his findings, and Nikki listened for any pertinent information. A few minutes later, Nikki's phone rang. It was the number Andrew had given her.

"It's Andrew," she told Hawk. He and the chief perked up. They told her to answer it and put it on speaker phone.

"Hello?" Nikki said.

"Nikki," Andrew whispered. "You have to come and help me. I'm surrounded. Why are there cops outside my motel room pointing guns at me? What happened with Karissa? Did she contact you? What's going on? I am freaking out."

"What do you mean, *surrounded*? Where are you? We've been trying to reach you all afternoon," Nikki said.

"There are cops outside of my hotel room."

Just then the chief's cell rang. It was an officer informing him that they had located Andrew. The chief told them to stand down.

"Listen, Andrew, tell me where you are, and we will come and get you. No one wants to hurt you; we just want to talk to you. The chief has ordered the police to stand down," Nikki said.

"Okay, Nikki. I am at the Overlook on the highway."

"I know exactly where you are. What room are you in?"

"The one surrounded by the cops," Andrew sneered.

"Now is not the time for sarcasm, Andrew," Nikki scolded.

"Okay, just get here quick. I don't want to get shot."

"Fine, we will. Just stay in the room. And Andrew, did Karissa call you this morning?"

"No, I haven't heard from her. What is going on?"

"I'll let you know when we get there," Nikki told him.

Andrew hung up and Nikki looked at Hawk. "Let's go," said Hawk.

"Just so you know, I do not think he did this. He sounded genuinely confused that the police were there."

Hawk looked at her and said he understood.

The chief instructed his men to keep an eye on the room. "Do not let anyone in or out, but do not shoot. Hawk, bring him in."

Nikki and Hawk ran to his truck and started for the motel. Even though the motel was on the highway, there were many windy back roads they had to take. The trees had new bright green leaves on their branches, and the sun was shining oblivious to the darkness Nikki was feeling. The Overlook was a small motel run by a local family. It was a single story of rooms that were a bit shabby. It was a motel where people stopped for a night or two. Fortunately, it was not peak tourist season, so there weren't too many guests staying there. When they got to the Overlook, Nikki admitted Andrew had been right. It was obvious which room was his. Andrew's room was surrounded by police from their county and two surrounding counties. There were other guests gathered by the motel office. The owners were there handing out coffee and reassurances, trying to keep their guests happy during the raid. Hawk parked his truck, and they walked toward the police.

"Hey, Jim," Hawk said to the officer in charge.

"Hey, Hawk," he replied.

"Has anyone tried to enter or leave?"

"No, not since we've been here," said Jim.

"Okay, we are going to go in. The suspect is not considered armed or dangerous," he said and looked at Nikki, and she nodded in agreement.

"Okay," Jim said. He instructed the other officers to lower their weapons but be on alert. Hawk thanked him.

He and Nikki approached the room. Nikki knocked on the door. She told Andrew it was her and asked him to open the door. There was no answer. Hawk asked her to step aside.

"Andrew!" Hawk yelled. "Open the door and come out with your hands up!" Hawk had not drawn his weapon, but he wanted Andrew intimidated into opening the door. Nikki tried to look in the window, but the curtains were closed. She looked at Hawk.

"We'll have to break in," said Hawk. Nikki agreed. She wondered why Andrew had not come to the door. Maybe she was wrong about him. He might have turned darker after he had left her. Maybe he had continued drinking himself to sleep. At least he had not smelled like beer this afternoon at the park. That was one good sign.

A loud noise drew Nikki's thoughts back to the motel. Hawk had kicked in the door and entered the room. A quick search showed that Andrew was not inside. The room was a mess. There were food wrappers and clothing strewn around the floor. In addition, a couple of lamps had been knocked over, and the closet door stood open. Hawk was the first to notice the bullet holes in the wall.

"Look here," he told Nikki. Nikki flinched and looked on the floor. There was no sign of blood. Nikki ran to the bathroom.

She saw the small window above the sink was open. It was small but large enough for someone to squeeze out. "Come here!" she yelled to Hawk. He ran in with his gun drawn and saw the window. The razor and toothbrush from the sink were on the floor by the opposite wall. It appeared someone had crawled out the window. There was a mirror by the side of the sink. It had been shattered. The glass fragments were all over the sink and on the floor. Hawk ran out of the motel room, and Nikki looked out the window. She heard an engine revving. She decided to follow whoever climbed out of the window. Nikki found a towel and wrapped her hand in it. She put her hand on the sink, mindful of the glass, and started to boost herself up. Nikki hopped on the sink and put her foot through the open window. She balanced there and then she stuck her head and shoulders out. She stretched and got her feet on the lower sill. Nikki jumped to the ground. She landed well and ran toward the back parking lot. A beat-up truck was weaving towards her. Nikki jumped out of the way just in time. Whoever was driving had tried to hit her. Nikki looked in the rearview window of the truck and saw two men. The driver was steering with one hand and beating up the passenger with his other hand. The passenger managed to turn around and look out the back window. He saw Nikki and put his hand on the glass. He had blood dripping from his hand, nose, and eye. It was Andrew. Nikki got the license plate number of the truck, and when Hawk appeared she gave it to him. She told him it looked like someone had kidnapped Andrew. *This day is getting weirder and weirder*, thought Nikki. Hawk had brought his truck around from the front of the motel. The other police were just getting around back. They had been searching around the motel for Andrew when Hawk told them he was no longer in the room. Hawk told the police what had happened. He said he would call the chief, and he was sure the chief would be sending them orders soon. Hawk and Nikki hopped into Hawk's truck and drove out of the parking lot and down the road after the truck with Andrew in it. They drove down the road the truck had taken, but there was no sign of it or Andrew. Nikki and Hawk drove around the country roads for a while, but there was no sign of the other vehicle. Hawk phoned in the license number, and the chief put an APB out on the truck. Suddenly Nikki's phone buzzed. It was a message from Andrew. She read it to Hawk.

"I am being held hostage in a cabin somewhere. Please help me."

"Let me call the chief, and he can tell me any nearby abandoned cabins," Hawk suggested. "I know some, but he should have a record of them at the station. That is probably where that other man has taken Andrew." Nikki agreed. Hawk called the chief, and the chief gave Hawk a nearby address.

"I will also have men looking around at the other cabins," said the chief. "I have a list of them on the map over my desk."

"I thought you might. Thank you, Chief," said Hawk. Hawk then warned Nikki to buckle up. "This is going to be a bumpy ride," he said. Hawk drove another mile and turned into what appeared to be the side of the road. Hawk drove into the long grass, and after a few feet Nikki could discern a trail. The ride was bumpy, and Nikki almost hit her head a time or two. The trail was nothing but overgrown grass in some places and dried up dirt in others. Nikki would have never known there was a trail, let alone a cabin here. Hawk was right. It was a bumpy ride. Nikki held on tight as Hawk guided them toward the abandoned cabin. The road got bumpier, and outside, the light dimmed as they got deeper into the woods. Nikki shivered. She wondered how scared Andrew was. Nikki knew what it was like to feel helpless. She felt a bit sorry for Andrew, but then she figured he had somehow done this to himself. Was the man a friend of Karissa's? Had he followed Andrew to Maple Hills? Had he seen Andrew shoot Karissa and followed him back to his hotel? Nikki's head was spinning with questions only Andrew could answer. She put her hand on Hawk's leg to steady herself. Hawk was busy maneuvering around the trail, but he shot her a reassuring smile. Nikki felt the truck lurch again and braced herself for the bump. She felt the truck slowing and realized they were stopping in the middle of the woods. There was nothing around but trees and some wildlife. There was no sign of a cabin. Nikki wondered where Hawk had taken her.

8

"The cabin is about a quarter of a mile away," Hawk told Nikki. Hawk stopped the car. He and Nikki got out. They were in dense woods surrounded by trees. It was darker and cooler in the woods. *At a better time, this would be a fun place to go with Hawk,* Nikki thought. She imagined hiking along the small trail and making new trails with Hawk. She pulled her mind back to the current situation.

"How do we get to the cabin?" Nikki asked Hawk.

"See that small trail?" he answered, pointing out a worn spot about a foot across that stretched into the woods.

"Yes," said Nikki.

"It's along that trail," replied Hawk. Nikki started walking, and Hawk followed closely behind.

They walked carefully, trying to avoid fallen logs and ruts in the ground. Nikki stopped and pointed. There was a deer a few yards ahead of them. While Nikki wanted to get to the cabin quickly, she did not want the deer spooked. Someone in the cabin might notice it running. She and Hawk stood there for a moment, and the deer wandered on after nibbling some young leaves. Hawk took the lead and moved through the woods, careful to be quiet. The woods were so still it seemed any noise would travel quite a distance. A cricket started chirping, and Nikki jumped. She kept up with Hawk along the trail. Suddenly, Hawk stopped. He motioned Nikki to his side.

"Look up ahead," he murmured to her.

"Where am I supposed to be looking?" Nikki asked. Hawk pointed up and Nikki saw a roof peak in the distance between the trees. She would not have noticed it if Hawk had not pointed it out. It was the same color as the tree trunks. Nikki figured the cabin must have been about as old as some of the trees. It now blended in with the forest.

"Follow me," said Hawk. Nikki followed right behind Hawk, careful not to make any noise or step off the trail. The sides of the trail were grown up, and Nikki did not want to step on anything she could not see. Hawk picked up the pace and as they got closer, the woods thinned a bit. The cabin was small and worn down. There were a few small windows. One of them appeared cracked. There was no sign of the truck. Nikki pointed that out to Hawk.

"They could have parked the truck further away," suggested Hawk. Nikki nodded. Hawk moved slowly toward the back of the cabin. Nikki followed. Hawk got to the side of one window and looked in. He shook his head and moved aside. Nikki looked in. There was an old wooden table and a chair and a lot of dirt and dust. It looked as if no one had been in that room for years. If

Andrew was in this cabin, he was not in that room. Hawk moved toward the side of the cabin. He looked in the window and shook his head again. Nikki looked in. There was a kitchen that had obviously not been used by any human being in quite a long time. There was an open cabinet with boxes strewn around the floor and some canisters on their sides. There was no food to be seen, and Nikki supposed it had been eaten by some critters. Everything in the room had a thick layer of dust. Hawk walked around to the front door and found it open. Nikki figured that is how the critters would have gotten in. Hawk walked in with his gun drawn. Nikki followed him and looked around. This was an old fishing cabin. A few stuffed fish hung on the wall, and there was an old cot in the corner of one of the rooms. There was room for one or two people to live here comfortably for a week at most. The only prints on the floor were from raccoons and other forest animals that now called this cabin home.

"I guess the raccoons enjoyed the food," Nikki said as they walked through the kitchen. They searched the cabin, but there was no sign of anyone ever being there. Nikki opened a closet and was startled by a squirrel that had made a nest there. Nikki jumped and shut the door quickly. She walked back to the front of the cabin. She noticed the cabin was not wired for electricity. She asked Hawk about that. He explained that this was one of the older fishing cabins. The man that owned it would use candles and lanterns to light the cabin.

"They came out here to fish, not watch television," Hawk explained.

Nikki remembered a cabin Andrew had rented outside

of Atlanta by a large lake. They had rented it before Seth was born. The area was quiet, but the cabin had a television, refrigerator, stove, and shower. Nikki preferred that cabin to this one. Thinking about Andrew made Nikki worry more. She turned to Hawk and voiced her concern.

"Now where do we go?" asked Nikki. She was starting to worry about Andrew. Yes, she did not like him, but she didn't want Seth's father getting hurt. Or, if he did get hurt, she wanted to be the one to inflict the pain.

Hawk came back toward the front door. "Let me check in with the chief. I seem to remember another cabin nearby." Hawk pulled out his cell, but there was no reception.

"We'll have to get back to the car to call him," Hawk said.

"What about your radio?" Nikki asked.

"I left it in the car. I didn't want it to go off while we were approaching the house."

"That makes sense," said Nikki. She and Hawk started back toward the car. Suddenly, Nikki heard a rattle. It sounded like a baby's rattle but more intense and close by her feet. She stopped. Hawk had heard it, too. He stopped and they looked around. Nikki knew that sound from hikes she had gone on. That was the sound of an angry rattlesnake. They needed to find the snake so they could avoid stepping on it. Hawk pointed about a foot off the trail. There was the snake, poised to strike. On the end of the tail was its rattle. It was shaking it hard trying to scare the humans away. Nikki knew if they continued down that trail, one or both of them would be bit. Hawk took Nikki's hand. He led her off the trail in the other direction about three feet. They walked in a half circle and got back on the trail about five feet from the snake. The snake settled back down, and Nikki and Hawk walked back to the car.

"That was too close," said Nikki.

"I can take you back to the station if you want me to. These deep woods can have some unpleasant creatures in them. Someone told me they saw a bear here once. As close as the trees are here, I believe him. If you don't want to be out here, I can find this guy on my own," said Hawk.

"No. I want to go with you. I just don't want to get bit by a poisonous snake or by a bear," Nikki replied.

"Okay. Let me call the chief." Hawk and Nikki climbed into his truck. He got on his radio and called his father.

"We checked the cabin, Chief. There was no one there." Hawk talked to the chief for a few more minutes.

Hawk hung up and started the truck. "The chief agreed that we should go to the next cabin. It's only about five miles from here."

"Is the road there any better?" Nikki asked. Hawk laughed.

"Nope," he replied. He turned the truck around and they bounced down to the road. Hawk asked how Nikki was holding up. She said she was fine. She told him she was still being objective; however, she was concerned that they had not found Andrew yet. Hawk reassured her that they would find him soon. He reminded her that the chief had different patrols checking out all the nearby cabins. About four miles later, Hawk pulled the truck off the road into what appeared to be high grass again. As they drove deeper into the woods, the tall grass disappeared, and shorter grass and moss surrounded them. The trees were just as thick here as they were by the other cabin. Hawk pulled the truck off the trail. Hawk stopped the truck before they could see the cabin. He got out of the truck and told Nikki to follow him. They walked along a small path that was just discernible through the undergrowth. At one point, they crossed a small stream. It was a bit too wide to hop across. Hawk helped Nikki across a stone path. Nikki was glad her feet were still dry when she reached the other side. She followed Hawk to where the trees thinned. Hawk stopped. He pointed, and Nikki looked. She saw a truck. It looked like the same truck that had almost run her over at the motel. She nodded to Hawk. The woods stopped, and there was a small meadow. On the other side was the cabin. This was a larger cabin. The front door was closed.

"We cannot approach from the front; there's no cover," said Hawk. "We'll have to follow the tree line to the back. The forest is close to the back porch. We can check in those windows first." Nikki agreed. She followed Hawk. This took longer than Nikki had anticipated. There was no trail, and they had to be careful of fallen trees and holes that animals had dug. Nikki stepped in one of the holes and turned her ankle. Hawk caught her.

"You should go back to the truck," he said.

"I'll be alright. It was just a quick turn," she reassured him.

"Okay," said Hawk, and they started walking again. Hawk helped Nikki over a fallen tree and under some low hanging branches. After what seemed like hours, they reached the back porch. It was a small porch that could fit about three or four people. There were three steps on the side leading up to the porch. There was a small bit of grass, but Hawk had been right. They had forest cover almost to the porch steps.

"Let me go first," said Hawk. He ducked and carefully walked slowly up the back porch stairs. He looked in the windows and motioned for Nikki to follow him. She carefully ascended the three steps. She ducked down beside Hawk and looked in the room. It was empty. Nikki could see the front door, and there was enough light from the other windows to realize no one was there. Nikki was getting very concerned. Andrew and the stranger should have been there. Nikki was sure that was the truck she had seen at the hotel.

"Where are they?" she whispered to Hawk.

"I'm not sure. We should go around and check the side windows." Nikki agreed. She and Hawk started to stand up. Just as Hawk and Nikki rose up to move to the side, the front door opened and a man walked into the cabin. He looked toward the back porch. Hawk pulled Nikki back down just in time.

9

Hawk pressed his finger to his lips. Nikki kept quiet. They listened outside the porch window. Nikki adjusted her feet and craned her neck so she could hear what was being said.

"So, Andrew, are you tired of running yet?" Nikki heard a strong New York accent coming from the cabin.

"What do you mean, running? Why am I here?" asked Andrew.

"I told you why. My boss is on his way. It would be easier if you went along with me. I don't know why you insist that you don't know him."

"Who is your boss?" Andrew asked.

"Mr. King," the man said.

"I don't know any Mr. King," Andrew insisted. There was a thud and a noise like air exhaling rapidly. Nikki tried to get up, but Hawk held her down. He shook his head.

"I really don't want to keep hitting you. I wish you would just cooperate."

"I don't know what you're talking about," insisted Andrew.

"You do know, and you will tell me where it is."

"I have told you over and over; I don't have that kind of money."

"I'm sure Mr. King will not be happy to hear that," the New York accent replied. "Maybe you need some more incentive."

"No, no, please don't hit me again. I'll tell you what you want to know," Andrew gasped. There was silence.

"Well?" asked the man, "Where's the money?"

"I would tell you if I knew, but I don't. I don't know what money you're talking about. I don't know any Mr. King."

Nikki heard the sound of a gun being cocked. She tried to look, but Hawk held her down.

"Maybe this will jog your memory," the man said.

"Don't shoot me!" yelled Andrew. Nikki twisted, but Hawk held her firmly.

"You are lucky Mr. King wants you alive." She breathed a sigh of relief, now understanding the gun was only a fear tactic. Nikki and Hawk kept on listening. Nikki could hear Andrew whimpering. She didn't blame him; he'd just had a gun in his face.

"Mr. King wants to get back what you owe him."

"How can I give something back that I don't have? And who is Mr. King?" Nikki heard the other man pacing.

"You owe Mr. King a bunch of money. He has been waiting for you to come back East. He's at the airport right now. He'll be here in a few minutes."

Nikki looked at Hawk. She wished he had his radio.

She knew his cell phone wouldn't have reception here. Hawk was listening with his gun out of his holster.

"What are you talking about? How did he know where I was? Why would he care?"

"You owe him money. He wants his money back. You were smart to run to California; he couldn't get to you there. I'm surprised you came back East."

"How did this Mr. King know where I was?" Andrew asked.

"He kept tabs on you. I found out you were flying back East, and Mr. King sent me to meet you. That woman got in the way, though. She kept interfering with my plans. I had to shoot her."

"Karissa? You shot Karissa?" Andrew moaned.

"Was that her name? Yes. I shot her in the alley. I was going to grab you at the park, but the old lady started screaming. Can you believe my luck? I thought no one would find her for a few hours. That would have given me time to grab you and run. As it turned out, when she screamed she drew all sorts of attention to the alley. I had to get out of there. That's when I decided to wait in your hotel room."

"I didn't know you were there in the closet," Andrew said.

"Obviously," the other voice boomed. "You nearly knocked me out with that lamp, and you grabbed my gun! I'm just glad I had the silencer on the gun from when I shot Karissa, or the cops would have come in shooting, you idiot!" Nikki heard a firmer thud, and Andrew wailed; she suspected the man had hit Andrew with the barrel of his gun. "You were easy, though," the man said with a laugh. "One swing, and you were down. It was a pain getting you through that bathroom window, but I got you out just in time. I should have run that woman over at the hotel. She was lucky you grabbed the wheel. Who was that woman?"

"No one. I… I just didn't want her to get run over," Andrew replied.

Nikki slipped from Hawk's grasp and peeked over the windowsill. She could see the man standing in front of a table. She didn't see Andrew. Hawk tried to pull her down, but Nikki stayed. The man at the table took a step away, and Nikki finally saw Andrew. He was tied up and bleeding. She gasped. The man turned and fired a shot, just missing Nikki. Hawk got up but didn't fire. He didn't want to hit Andrew. Nikki started running off the porch. The man fired at Hawk, and the bullet managed to graze Hawk's gun, knocking it from his grasp. The man dashed out the back door and caught Hawk in a neck grasp, placing his gun to Hawk's head. Nikki froze.

"That's it, honey. Come back here slowly and carefully," the man said to Nikki. "If you don't, I'll put a bullet in his head."

Nikki turned around. Hawk was in a headlock, and the gun was right at his temple.

"Okay, just don't shoot him," she pleaded.

"I won't, yet," the gunman threatened. Nikki walked back to the porch and climbed up the stairs.

"Get into the cabin and sit by the table," the man ordered. Nikki did what he demanded. The man roughly dragged Hawk into the cabin. He sat him on a seat and had Nikki tie him up. The man then tied Nikki to the other chair. Andrew was watching the whole scene; his eyes seemed to apologize to Nikki when she sat down. Nikki just looked worried. *How are we going to get out of this*, she wondered.

"Are you okay?" she asked Andrew.

"Shut up," the man said. Andrew nodded quickly while the man was tying Nikki to the chair.

"You will never get away with this," said Hawk. "The police are on their way. They'll be here soon. It would be easier for you to just let us go now."

The man laughed. "What police?" he asked.

"The chief will be here. He and the other police who are out there looking for you will be here soon. There's a manhunt on for you," Nikki insisted.

"I don't believe that. Why would they bother looking for this guy?" he pointed at Andrew.

"They will be here soon," Hawk warned. The man scoffed and shook his head.

"We're safe," he said. "No one will find us out here."

Unfortunately, Nikki was starting to believe him.

10

Hawk, Nikki, and Andrew were sitting at a kitchen table. Their hands and feet were bound to the chairs. Up close, Andrew looked worse. It seemed to Nikki like he had been hit quite a bit. She told him everything was going to be okay. The man holding them hostage strode over. He threatened to hit Nikki. He told her to keep her mouth shut.

"Leave her alone," Hawk cried.

"What's it to you?" the man asked, clearly annoyed.

"I told you, the police are on their way. Things will go more smoothly for you if you let us go. You do not want to harm us."

"Don't tell me what I want to do," said the man, turning to Hawk. He backhanded Hawk and Nikki gasped.

"See," said the man. "That is what happens when you don't shut up."

Nikki looked at Hawk. There was blood trickling down his chin. She felt awful. *This is all my fault*, she thought. *I*

should not have dragged Hawk into any mess involving Andrew.
She closed her eyes and tried to think of a way out of the
situation. She felt a hand on her neck. The man jerked her
head up.

"I recognize you. You and police guy were at the park
today with Andrew. What were you doing there?"

Nikki did not answer him. She looked at him defiantly.
The man shrugged and turned to Hawk. He hit him again,
hard. Nikki still didn't say anything. Tears were rolling
down her cheeks, but she didn't say a word. She didn't
want to give this man any information.

"So, you two won't answer me?" he questioned and
then gave Nikki a taunting stare. "Didn't your mama tell
you it's not polite to ignore someone?"

"Didn't your mama tell you not to hurt people?" Nikki
said. The man frowned and raised his fist.

"Don't!" yelled Hawk as the man's fist hit Nikki's
cheek.

Nikki felt her head snap back quickly. The back of her
head hit something. She saw stars and then darkness. She
heard Andrew and Hawk yelling, but she could not make
out what they were saying. She opened her eyes at last and
saw the ceiling. Hawk was trying to break out of the chair.
Andrew was yelling at the man. The man leaned over
Nikki. She could feel his breath on her face.

"Are you ready to talk now?" he asked. Nikki did not
answer him. Her whole head was throbbing, and the room
was spinning. The man pulled his foot back and kicked
Nikki in the ankle. She gasped and cried out. Hawk
roared, "Stop!"

"How about you? Are you ready to talk now?" the man asked Hawk.

"Yes. Just please stop hurting her," Hawk said between clenched teeth.

The man lifted Nikki and her chair. He sat her upright. Nikki clenched her teeth but did not cry. "Don't tell him anything, Hawk," she pleaded.

The man turned to her. "You're stronger than you look. What is it they say down south, maybe I'll have to break this filly?"

He grabbed Nikki's hair and Hawk yelled at him.

"We were meeting Andrew to talk about Karissa!" Hawk cried.

"That's better," said the man, letting go of Nikki's hair and stroking it. She cringed at his touch. The room was steadying itself slowly. A wave of nausea washed over Nikki, but she gulped some air and held it down. *I probably have a concussion*, she thought. *I must have hit my head on the wall when he hit me.* She heard Hawk talking and tried to listen to what he was saying.

"Yes, we were meeting Andrew to talk about Karissa, the woman you killed," Hawk said.

"Oh, you heard that?" the man asked. "That's too bad. We'll see what Mr. King wants to do with you now that you know what I've done. Why would you want to talk to Andrew about Karissa?"

"Because she wanted me dead," said Nikki.

The man laughed. "I guess I took care of that problem for you." Nikki cringed. "What, no thank you?" The man laughed and stroked Nikki's hair again, firmly. He looked her over. "Why did I find you outside this cabin?" the man asked Nikki.

Nikki wanted to reply, but the nausea hit her again. She looked at Hawk pleadingly.

"I'll tell you," said Hawk. The man turned to face Hawk, but he kept his hand on Nikki's neck.

"This had better be the truth, or I will hurt her again," the man threatened. Hawk kept his composure. Nikki felt like throwing up on the guy's shoes but thought better of it. She gulped for more air.

"Andrew texted us when you took him. He told us you were holding him in a cabin. We started searching for you as soon as we got the text. This is the second cabin we searched."

"How did you get a text out?" the man asked Andrew.

"I did it when you left me in the truck to search the cabin. You had me tied up, but I managed to grab the phone and send out one text. I threw the phone out of the truck before you came back. When you searched me, it was gone."

The man moved toward Andrew.

"Don't," Nikki pleaded.

Just then they all heard a car approaching. The man told them to be quiet or he would hit them again. As they waited, they heard three car doors open and slam shut. Heavy feet were heard on the front porch. Nikki, Hawk, and Andrew waited quietly while the man moved toward the front window. *I hope it's the police*, Nikki thought. Her hopes were dashed when the man turned around, smiling.

"Mr. King is here," he announced.

As the man stepped back from the window, two armed men came through the front door. They were tall, well-muscled, and well-armed. They took their places beside the door. Behind them was another man. After he entered, the bodyguards shut the cabin door. The man who entered behind them was tall and intimidating, too. He didn't carry a gun, and he was wearing a designer suit with heavy gold chains. His dark hair was combed back, and when he smiled at the man holding them hostage, Nikki noticed he had a gold tooth. There were heavy gold rings on his fingers, and Nikki guessed they were not just for show. She looked over at Andrew. He looked pale.

"What have you gotten us in to?" she hissed.

"I don't know who that is," insisted Andrew. Nikki rolled her eyes. The man who had taken Andrew walked over to the tall man. He shook his hand.

"Hello, Mr. King," said the man.

"Hello, Jim," said Mr. King. "Why do we have three hostages? Which one is Andrew?"

"I was holding Andrew, and these other two thought they would be heroes," explained Jim. "The one in the suit is Andrew."

Mr. King glanced at Nikki and Hawk. He shook his head, and then he turned and stared at Andrew. He walked over and hit Andrew with a closed fist. Andrew whimpered. Mr. King took out a handkerchief and wiped off his hand.

"Let me tell you a story, Andrew," Mr. King began as he slowly paced around the room. "Quite a few years ago, you were living in New York. I'm not sure why you chose New York, and I only learned later that you had come from Atlanta. You enjoyed living in my city. You gambled and had some fun with some women. One day you gambled a bit too much, didn't you?" he stopped pacing and looked at Andrew. Andrew looked sullen and confused. Mr. King continued. "You needed some help. You went to a shop recommended by your bookie. That shop was owned by me."

Andrew looked up suddenly and turned paler than he already was.

"Ah, it seems you're getting your memory back. For those in the room that are still confused, let me continue. Andrew went to the shop and told his tale of woe. My associate agreed to loan him the money. All Andrew had to do was deliver some packages around the city for me. He didn't have to pay the money back. Andrew thought this was a fair deal and arrangements were made to pay off his debts. Andrew was given times and places to pick up and drop off my packages. Andrew completed his tasks in a timely manner, and we called it a day. That would have been the end of the story. It's a nice story, no? We have the down-and-out man working to make his debts go away. We have me, the generous businessman who agreed to help him. Debts were paid, and the story ends. Right? Well, it seems that Andrew has a bit of a gambling problem. Instead of being happy with his debts being paid off and leaving the city, he decided to stay and start gambling again. Sure enough, he got himself into trouble again. He went to see my associate, and my associate told him it would be the same deal, although this time he would have more deliveries. Andrew agreed, and my associate paid off his debts. This would have been fine, except Andrew decided he didn't want to work for my money this time. He skipped town. I have been waiting for him to show his face back East. I'm confident I won't be getting my money back from him, so it seems I'm going to have to make an example out of him."

Nikki was listening to what Mr. King was saying. She felt nauseous and angry at Andrew. How dare he put her and Hawk in this situation! She looked over at Andrew. His head was hanging down, and she knew what Mr. King had said was true.

"What were you thinking?" she cried out to Andrew.

"I wasn't," he mumbled in reply. "I didn't want to deliver his packages again. The last time I delivered one, something happened at the delivery point the next day; it was raided by cops. I didn't know what I was delivering, but I figured it was probably something illegal."

Hawk was listening to all this shaking his head. "What

did you think would happen?" he asked Andrew. "Did you think your problems would disappear when you went to California?"

"Actually, yes," Andrew replied. "I hadn't heard anything about this debt until now. I figured if they hadn't come after me by now then I was in the clear."

Mr. King shook his head. He paced around the room and turned towards Andrew. "Not too smart," Mr. King said. "So, the question now is, how do I do it? What would make up for all of the running you did? Should I just shoot you in the head, or should I make it hurt? Maybe I will make it last. I could start with breaking some fingers or a hand and then shoot you in the kneecaps. We're a long way from anyone out here. Do you think anyone will hear you scream?" Mr. King bent over Andrew. He spit the last words in Andrew's face. He grabbed Andrew by the hair.

"Wait," said Nikki and Hawk. Mr. King let go of Andrew's hair. He turned toward Nikki and Hawk.

"What business of yours is this anyway? Why did you come out here looking for him? Does he owe you money, too?" Mr. King asked.

"No, he doesn't," Nikki confessed. "I'm his ex-wife." Mr. King raised his eyebrows.

"Are you from New York? I don't remember hearing about you," he said.

"No. I'm from Atlanta."

"That's surprising. What are you doing up here?" Mr. King asked.

"Andrew walked out on me one night. He abandoned me. I moved up here to start a new life and get away from

Atlanta." Nikki purposefully did not tell Mr. King about Seth or the shop. The less he knew, the better.

"Who is this guy?" Mr. King pointed at Hawk.

"He's a friend of mine. He came along to help me find Andrew," Nikki explained.

"He's the one that said the police are coming," Jim said.

"What police?" Mr. King asked.

"Don't worry, I checked out the department. It's small. They're still trying to find this cabin. We'll be out of here before they show up," reassured Jim. Mr. King smiled.

"I'm glad you did your homework," he said to Jim. "Now, where was I? Oh yes, let's break some fingers, boys." The guards took a step away from the door. Andrew was shaking his head over and over.

"Wait," Nikki said to Mr. King. His guards stopped and looked at him. "How much money does Andrew owe you?"

"I wouldn't worry about that, darling. It's out of your price range," Mr. King replied.

"Humor me," Nikki demanded.

"Oh, a feisty one?" Mr. King asked as he approached Nikki's chair. He took her chin in his hand and tilted her face up to his. Nikki frowned, and Mr. King laughed. "Okay, I'll tell you. He owes me $10,000."

"I have that," said Nikki. Mr. King looked at her. He bent his face close to hers. "No, you don't. You're lying, trying to buy time."

"I am not lying," Nikki said, looking right into Mr. King's red–rimmed eyes. "Take me into town, and I will get it for you."

"I don't believe you," Mr. King said.

"It's true. Check my account. You'll see it's all there."
Mr. King let go of Nikki's chin. She maintained eye contact
with him.

"You have $10,000?" Mr. King asked.

"Yes. Take me to town, and it's all yours." Nikki never
took her eyes off of Mr. King. She wanted his attention to
be on her, not Andrew.

"Why would you help this creep? He abandoned you,"
said Mr. King, sneering at Andrew.

"Despite what he's done, I don't want him to die," said
Nikki.

Mr. King paced a bit and turned to Jim. "Do you have a
cell phone?"

"Yes, Mr. King."

"What is the bank's number?" Mr. King asked Nikki.

"It is 555-257-2575," said Nikki.

"Jim, dial that number and see what happens," Mr.
King commanded. He looked at Andrew, Hawk, and
Nikki. "I do not want any funny business. No speaking
out of line. Do not scream. Do not tell them what is
happening here. If you do, I will kill you."

Jim dialed the number and put the phone on speaker.

"Thank you for calling First United Bank, how can I
direct your call?" Mr. King looked at Nikki. He signaled
her to speak.

"Hi Jenna, this is Nikki," she said.

"Hi Nikki, what can I do for you?"

"I would like to check my savings account balance."

"Sure thing, Nikki, hold on just a minute." The phone
was put on hold. Mr. King threatened to kill Hawk and
Andrew if Nikki tried anything. She said she understood.

Jenna got back on the line. Nikki gave Jenna her password and account information. Jenna told her she had a balance of $12,000.

"Is there anything else I can help you with?" Jenna asked Nikki.

"No, thank you, Jenna," Nikki replied. She wanted to scream for help, but she knew that would not end well. Jenna ended the call, and Jim put the phone back in his pocket.

Nikki looked at Mr. King. "I will give it all to you. All you have to do is let us go," she said. "Andrew was my husband and I loved him, once. We had a good life in Atlanta. Andrew skipped out on me. I didn't know where he had gone. I was devastated. I decided to move to Maple Hills to start over. Andrew has a life in California, and I have one here. Just let us live our lives, please," she begged Mr. King.

Mr. King had been listening. He cocked his head and thought for a moment.

"There's a problem with your story," he said. "Why would you move to a small town up north? Why didn't you move somewhere else? No. I don't believe you. I think what happened," and here Mr. King looked right at Nikki, "is this: Andrew and you did not split up. You moved up here when he was in New York. He gave you some of my money. That is how you have that much cash in your savings account. You stole from me, too. That's why you've been living up here. I'm surprised we didn't know about you. You covered your tracks well."

"That is not it at all!" said Nikki. "I covered my tracks because I didn't want Andrew to find me. I didn't know why he left, but I was sure it was something I didn't want to be involved in. I have saved up my money on my own. I did not steal from you. Like I said, this is the first time I've seen Andrew since he walked out on me." Nikki ended this by glaring at Andrew.

"She's telling the truth," Andrew said. "I haven't seen her since I left her in Atlanta. The stuff in New York was all my doing. Please don't hurt her. It's me you want. Do whatever you want to me. Take her money and let her and her friend go."

"That is tempting," said Mr. King, turning on his heel and pacing away from the group. He turned around. "But no. It's too late. Your friends have seen me. Sure, I'll get her money on my way out of town. I can be persuasive when it comes to bank tellers." His guards chuckled. "I don't need any of you. You have taken up enough of my time. Now, hand me your gun," he said to Jim. Jim handed him his gun. "I will shoot Andrew. After that, you can take care of these two. Now, untie them and let's get this over with." His bodyguards walked over and helped Jim untie the hostages. Hawk tried to get up, but the bodyguard held him down. Mr. King turned around. "It's a pity. You are kind of cute," he said to Nikki as he pointed the gun at Andrew's head. Just then, there was a loud noise, and the door burst open.

12

T he door broke in, and the guards jumped back. It was the SWAT team. They rushed in. Andrew and Hawk stood up. They both tried to get to the bodyguards. The SWAT team yelled and aimed their guns at the guards, Jim, and Mr. King. Mr. King dove for Nikki. Nikki had started to get up and felt nauseous again. She had sat back down. Next thing she knew she was being lifted from the chair. She could feel a large arm around her neck. Mr. King had grabbed her and had the gun pointed at her head.

"Everyone stop," he commanded. "I have a hostage. I will shoot her. Let me walk out of here, and I will think about letting her go." He pulled Nikki toward the back porch door. Nikki regained her footing. She looked at Hawk. She smiled and winked at him. Hawk smiled back. Nikki raised her right foot and brought it down hard on Mr. King's loafers. Mr. King yelled and let go of Nikki. He dropped his gun. Hawk ran over and tackled him. Nikki grabbed Mr. King's gun and pointed it at him. Hawk then quickly threw some cuffs on Mr. King. The SWAT team put the others in cuffs. At that moment, the chief walked in. He saw Hawk and walked over to him.

"Are you okay, son?"

"Yes, Dad, I am okay. Here," he shoved Mr. King toward the chief. "I cuffed him for you." The chief smiled and hauled Mr. King out of the room. Nikki gave Mr. King's gun to the police. She turned around and saw Andrew. She walked over to him. Andrew opened his arms as though he honestly believed she would hug him. Nikki stopped, reached up her arm, and slapped him. She turned around and walked over to Hawk.

"I'm ready to leave now," she declared. Hawk smiled and took her hand. They walked out in the woods to his truck.

"Hey, how about me?" yelled Andrew.

"Get a ride from one of the cops," suggested Hawk.

"Yeah, you deserve to be in the back of a cruiser," said Nikki. Andrew's shoulders slumped, and he walked over to the police. One officer said he would give him a ride, and he stuck him in the back of the car. Nikki and Hawk smiled, and they continued on their way to Hawk's truck.

"You know, you were very brave back there," said Hawk.

"Thank you," said Nikki. "I was scared out of my wits. I cannot believe Andrew brought that into Maple Hills."

"It's okay," Hawk soothed her and stopped. He held her close and kissed her.

Nikki relaxed in Hawk's arms. "Well, we need to go to the station," she said. "The chief will want our statements," she said.

"Okay," said Hawk. "We can get someone to look at your head while we're there."

"That sounds good," said Nikki, instinctively reaching to touch the back of her head where she had hit. "I have a wicked headache."

Hawk opened the truck door for her. He helped her in. They drove down to the station where they were met with police and SWAT vehicles. Hawk parked near the station and got out of the truck. He helped Nikki out, and they went into the precinct. Andrew was there waiting, and he got up when they came in. Andrew started to walk towards Nikki, but he was interrupted.

"Mom!" Seth called out, darting right past his father without even noticing the man's presence. He walked over to Nikki and gave her a gentle hug. "What happened? Where's Dad?" Nikki said it was a long story, and she nodded towards Andrew. Seth spun around, realizing he had walked right by him. Andrew smiled at Seth and held his arms open. Seth just shook his head and walked away. Nikki felt a lump of pride in her throat, but she was still saddened because she knew Andrew's presence alone was enough to hurt Seth. She swallowed her tears and wiped her eyes. The chief walked over.

"We're ready to take your statements."

"I'll go first," Andrew pushed ahead. Hawk stopped him.

"No. Nikki goes first. She needs to see a doctor," he insisted. Andrew agreed and sat down. Nikki thanked Hawk and followed the chief back into the interrogation room.

Later, after Nikki had seen a doctor and everyone had given their statements, the FBI appeared. The chief said they wanted to talk to Andrew some more. Hawk and Nikki waited while the FBI talked to him. Nikki was sitting down by the chief's desk when Andrew walked back in. A bureau officer was with him.

"Usually, we do this in private, but Andrew wanted you to hear this," said the bureau officer. He closed the door and sat down by Nikki. Andrew and Hawk remained standing in the room. "We have offered Andrew a deal," the officer said. "If he testifies against Mr. King, any charges he has coming will be dropped. Now, this will involve witness protection." Nikki looked up at Andrew.

"I want to take the offer," he said. "I'm just concerned about Seth."

"Seth will be fine here with us," said Nikki. "Hawk and I will keep him safe."

"Okay," Andrew agreed. "Can I talk to him? The officer said we have to leave soon. I... I might never see him again. I have some things I want to say."

"I'm not sure," said Nikki. "He didn't want to talk to you earlier."

"Please, can you just ask him? Everyone can be in the room. I just want to apologize," Andrew pleaded. Hawk reassured Nikki he would be there.

Nikki agreed and went to look for Seth. She found him talking to an FBI agent.

"Hey, Mom, I was just telling this agent about grandpa," Seth said. Nikki smiled. Her father had worked for the FBI. Nikki had attended the academy until she and Andrew had gotten married.

"Seth, your father wants to talk to you."

"I don't want to talk to him," Seth replied with a frown.

"I understand. I need you to know that Hawk and I will be in the room with you. You don't have to talk to him, but I think it might be a good idea. If you feel uncomfortable or want to leave, that's fine. I will not keep you there."

"Okay. I'll go, but if he says one bad thing about you, I am out of there."

"If he says one bad thing about us, you'll probably have to hold Hawk back," Nikki said and laughed. Seth laughed with her. They walked back to the chief's office. The chief was at his desk.

"Hawk took Andrew to interrogation room one," he informed Nikki. "He said you could meet them there."

"Thank you, Chief."

Nikki and Seth walked to the interrogation room. Hawk was standing, and Andrew was sitting. Nikki motioned to the seat across from Andrew, and Seth sat down. Nikki walked over to Hawk and leaned on him. He put his arm around her, and they listened to Andrew.

Andrew had tears in his eyes. "Seth, you have grown up to become a wonderful man," he said. Andrew continued, "I am so proud of you. Your mother has done a fine job raising you despite my actions. I wanted you to know that I'm sorry. What I did was wrong and unforgivable. I love you, Seth, and I want only good things for you."

Seth kept quiet while Andrew talked. He stared at

Andrew. When he was sure Andrew was done, he said, "I forgive you, Dad, but I never want to see you again." He looked at Nikki. She nodded. He got up and walked out. Andrew had tears running down his face. He wiped them off and turned to Nikki.

"Thank you," he said. "Hawk, could you ask the FBI agent to come in? I'm ready to leave now." Hawk looked at Nikki, and she nodded. He opened the door and stuck his head out and asked the officer to come in.

Meanwhile, Andrew spoke to Nikki. "I am so sorry for everything I have done. I never should have walked out on you. I was and am a coward."

Nikki looked at him. "What you're doing right now is brave," she reassured him. "You're leaving to protect your son."

Andrew thanked her and told the FBI agent he was ready to go. As he walked by Hawk, Andrew thanked him and said he was confident Hawk would keep Nikki and Seth safe before he left with the agent.

Hawk held Nikki close. She felt tired suddenly and said she needed to sit down. Hawk helped her to the chair and pulled the other one around across from her. He held her hands in his.

"Nikki, let's go out to dinner tonight. I think we have both earned a nice night out on the town. What do you think?"

Nikki smiled. It wasn't often that Hawk suggested dinner out. Usually he cooked for her. She thought about it and said she wanted to check with Seth first. Hawk left her there and found Seth. Nikki told Seth that Hawk wanted to take her out to dinner.

"I know this has been a rough day. If you want, I'll stay at home with you tonight," Nikki said.

"Thank you, Mom, but you should go out. You and Hawk deserve a nice night out. Tori offered to make me dinner. She wants to stay at her place and play some games and just be together. I told her I would if you didn't need me."

Nikki laughed. Seth was a wonderful son. "Thank you, but I should be fine with Hawk."

"Okay," said Seth. "Tori will be happy." Seth smiled and bounded away. Hawk helped Nikki up.

"Let me take you home, and you can get a shower and get changed," Hawk suggested.

"That sounds like a plan," said Nikki. She was looking forward to a hot shower and a nice dinner out. She hugged and kissed Hawk. "What would I do without you?" she asked.

"You'd be just fine. You are one tough lady." Hawk smiled at Nikki and took her hand. "I will drop you by the house and pick you up by six. How does that sound?"

"That sounds wonderful," Nikki said. She smiled, and they walked together to Hawk's truck.

13

Nikki got into the shower. It felt good to wash the day off. She flinched as the water hit her face and head. She didn't feel dizzy or nauseous anymore, and the medicine the doctor had given her had taken away her headache. She got out of the shower, and she looked in her closet. She picked out a red dress. It was short and sleeveless. She put on some red pumps and gently applied her makeup. She heard Hawk downstairs and quickly put on some earrings. As she walked down the steps, Hawk whistled.

"You look stunning," he said. He helped her with her shawl. Nikki took his arm, and Hawk led her to his truck.

"Where are we going?" Nikki asked.

"It's a surprise," said Hawk.

"A surprise?" asked Nikki.

"Yes."

"Can I guess?" she asked.

"No," Hawk said. Nikki knew Hawk was no good at keeping secrets. She knew if she asked him questions she would figure out where they were going. She decided not to pester him that night, so she stretched and relaxed in her seat. Hawk smiled. They drove into town, and Hawk parked by the only gourmet restaurant in Maple Hills.

"Wow, what's the occasion?" Nikki asked.

"Why do I need an occasion to take you out to dinner?" Hawk asked as he helped her down from the truck. He pulled her close and kissed her. "My occasion is that I have a beautiful woman on my arm. I want to show you off," he said. Nikki laughed. She walked with him into the restaurant. *I suppose surviving the world's worst encounter with your girlfriend's ex is worth celebrating,* Nikki mused. They were seated immediately. The waiter brought over some wine. Nikki smiled as the waiter uncorked it at the table.

"Did you order this?" Nikki asked Hawk.

"Yes, I did," he said, smiling.

Nikki smiled. Hawk was usually a beer kind of guy, but he enjoyed a good wine, too. She sipped from the glass the waiter handed her. It was delicious.

"You have good taste," Nikki told Hawk.

"Thank you, ma'am," he replied, still smiling at her.

The waiter came over with a cheese platter. "Did you order that, too?" Nikki asked Hawk.

"Yep. Your dinner is taken care of tonight," Hawk said. Nikki was excited. She could not wait to see what was coming next.

"You were very brave today," Hawk said, taking Nikki's hand.

"Thank you, but I could not have done it without you," she said.

"We make a good team."

"Yes, we do," Nikki agreed.

The next course was a spring greens salad with homemade dressing. Nikki ate it all, enjoying the spiciness of the greens and the sweetness of the dressing. After the salad came the main course. Hawk had ordered lobster risotto for both of them. It was rich and creamy. Nikki savored every bite.

"I'm full," she told Hawk.

"I hope not," he said.

Just then the waiter appeared with dessert.

"This is a special dessert we made for the happy couple," the waiter said. Nikki looked at Hawk. He smiled. The dessert was strawberries and cracked black pepper in a champagne flute. Hawk pierced a strawberry and fed it to Nikki.

"Yum," she said. "That is incredible."

They enjoyed their dessert. After dinner, Hawk suggested they walk to the park.

"That is a great idea," said Nikki. "I have to walk off this rich food."

"You don't have to walk anything off," Hawk said, looking her up and down. Nikki laughed. They walked hand-in-hand slowly to the gazebo. There was a bench in the gazebo, and Hawk suggested they sit down. Nikki agreed. They sat in silence for a few minutes. Nikki was enjoying the fresh air. It was a bit nippy, but with Hawk beside her, Nikki was comfortable.

"We've been through a lot together," said Hawk.

"Yes, we have," said Nikki. "And, that was just one day." She laughed.

Hawk put his hand gently on Nikki's cheek. She turned her head towards him, and he leaned in and kissed her. She smiled. *I feel so safe with Hawk*, she thought.

"I wanted to talk to you about something," Hawk said.

"What is that?" asked Nikki.

"Well, I've been thinking about something, but the time has just never been right. Sitting here tonight, I realized it may never be right. Trouble seems to follow us around."

Nikki started to feel worried. "Yeah, but we have had fun, too," she said.

Hawk agreed. "You're right. We have had a lot of fun together. Nikki." He paused and looked at her. "I have something to ask you."

"What is it?" she asked.

Hawk turned his body toward her and dropped to one knee in front of her. Nikki gasped.

"Nikki, I love you. I've loved you from the moment I first laid eyes on you. Sure, we've seen our share of trouble, but we've also survived. We've survived together. I'm happy because of you, and I want to be happy with you forever. Nikki, will you marry me?"

Nikki was crying by that point. Hawk let go of her hand and brought out a small box. He placed it in her hands. Nikki opened it. The ring was sapphire and emerald.

"This is gorgeous," she said to Hawk. She flung her arms around him, and he lifted her off the bench.

"Yes, yes, yes, I will marry you," Nikki nearly shouted. Hawk kissed her. He put the ring on her finger.

"I hope you don't mind," he said. "But, this was my mother's wedding ring. When I told the chief that I was going to propose, he gave it to me. He said it brought him and my mom many years of happiness, and he hoped it would do the same for us."

"It is perfect," sighed Nikki. She kissed Hawk again. *I'm getting married,* she thought giddily. Nikki could not stop smiling.

"I have to call Seth. He'll want to know about this," Nikki insisted.

"You don't have to call him," Hawk said.

"Oh, but I want to. I want him to be the first to hear about this."

"He is," said Hawk.

Nikki looked at him quizzically. Suddenly Seth was there. Nikki started crying again. Seth, Tori, Lidia and her husband, and the chief were all at the gazebo. Lidia had a bottle of champagne, and her husband had the glasses. Hawk popped the cork, and they all cheered. Lidia's husband passed champagne around to everyone. Nikki looked at Seth.

"You knew about this?" she asked.

"Yeah," Seth said. "Hawk asked me if he could marry you the other day when we went out to lunch. Of course, I said yes."

Nikki smiled. She didn't think she would ever stop smiling. *That was so nice of Hawk to ask Seth,* she thought.

"You are such a gentleman," she said to Hawk. He blushed.

Nikki turned to the chief. "Thank you for the beautiful ring," she said.

"You are welcome, Nikki. I wouldn't want anyone else to have it. You have made my son so happy. Thank *you,*" the chief replied. Nikki smiled. Lidia and Tori came over and hugged her.

"We're so happy for you," Lidia said.

"Did you know about this?" asked Nikki.

"Oh, totally, but Seth has known a lot longer than the rest of us," Tori told Nikki. Nikki thanked Lidia's husband and hugged Tori and Lidia again. She hugged Seth tight.

"Thank you for being such a wonderful human being," she said.

"Thank you for being the best mom ever," he returned. Nikki turned to Hawk.

"I cannot believe you pulled this off," she said.

"Some secrets are worth keeping," he replied. He grabbed Nikki and swung her gently around the gazebo. Nikki felt the breeze and danced with Hawk around and around. They stayed that way for a while, and then, as the others left, Nikki thanked them for being a part of her memorable night. She felt a bit let down as the tiredness took over. Hawk told her to sit down. He brought out a thermos. It was filled with hot coffee, just the way Nikki liked it. He produced two mugs and poured each of them a mug full. Hawk held up his mug in a toast gesture.

"Here's to us," he said. Nikki touched his mug with hers.

"Here's to us," she replied. They sat and sipped their coffee, looking at the stars.

"Are you done with your coffee yet?" Hawk asked.

"Yes, I am. Why? Is it time to go home?"

"Not quite," said Hawk, taking her hand and guiding her off her seat.

"What's going on?" asked Nikki.

"You'll see," said Hawk. He led her to his truck and helped her in. He got in beside her and started the engine.

"I've had this whole proposal planned for a while now," Hawk said as he steered his truck out of the town. "If I had known today was going to happen, I probably would have planned something different."

"What was wrong with the proposal?" Nikki asked. "I thought it was beautiful."

"I'm glad you liked that part. The next part maybe not so much. I talked to Seth, and he reassured me you would like it. So, I hope you like it and I apologize in advance."

"What are you talking about?" Nikki's curiosity was piqued.

"You'll see," said Hawk, driving down a windy road. He drove for about fifteen more minutes and then put his turn signal on. Nikki looked where he was turning. It was dark and overgrown.

"Where are we going?" she asked.

"Someplace I think you will like," replied Hawk. "I promise if you don't I will take you home."

"Okay," said Nikki. She trusted Hawk. This time when they turned off the road the trail they followed was not bumpy. It was smooth dirt and the trees filled in around it. It was a well-traveled trail, and Hawk seemed confident driving Nikki to their destination.

"Close your eyes," Hawk said after a few minutes.

"Okay," said Nikki. She closed her eyes. After a minute, Hawk stopped the truck.

"You can open your eyes now."

Nikki gasped in amazement. In front of her was a

gorgeous log cabin. There were white lights strung in the trees, and she could see a lamp on inside.

"It is beautiful," she cried.

"Come with me," Hawk said. He had gotten out of the truck and opened Nikki's door. She walked next to him holding his hand. They walked to the front door of the cabin, and Hawk opened the door. The interior was something out of a magazine. The logs were exposed, and the wooden floor was finished and clean. There was a full kitchen and a large living area on the first floor.

"There are three bedrooms upstairs," Hawk told Nikki.

"I didn't bring any change of clothes," she said.

"Seth and Tori took care of that. Tori even packed your bathing suit."

"Why would I need a bathing suit?" Nikki asked.

"For this," Hawk said as he opened up the back door. The back door led to a patio. It was large and there were steps leading down the other end. There were tall plants around the steps blocking off the view. Hawk took Nikki down the steps and she gasped. The steps led to the lake. There was a sandy shore and a boat launch. Beside the boat launch was a canoe. Nikki could not believe how beautiful it was. She was stunned.

"I love it," she said.

"I thought it would be nice to spend an evening by the lake. In fact, you and I are not due back in town for the rest of the week. Before you protest, I cleared this with Lidia. She said the timing was perfect. She was going to suggest closing the store for the week and re-opening it on Monday with its new features."

"New features?" Nikki asked.

"Yes," said Hawk. "Lidia and Tori were able to get everything you needed to open up the milkshake fountain. You will be serving milkshakes, egg creams, root beer floats, and homemade ice cream."

"Who's going to be making the ice cream if I'm here with you?" she asked Hawk.

"Tori and Seth are. Seth remembered your peach ice cream recipe. He called down to Atlanta the day you thought about this and ordered some local peaches. They arrived yesterday. Tori has been keeping them at her house. Seth made a batch of ice cream and brought it up to the cabin. Would you like to try some?"

Nikki was astounded. She could not believe her friends had pulled this off. She started to cry.

"Oh, I'm sure the ice cream is good," said Hawk. "If that's what you're worried about." He pulled Nikki into his arms. She felt safe and warm. He let her cry until she was done.

"You are one of the sweetest men I have ever met," she said to Hawk. "Yes, I would love to try Seth's ice cream. And then we can take a dip in the lake. I'm sure the water is cold, but I think it is just what I need."

"I will start a fire while we eat our ice cream so we can warm up when we get done swimming," Hawk suggested. Nikki loved the idea. She thought about her day and about Andrew. She thought about Seth, Tori, and Lidia. It was nice to be able to close one door and open another one in her life. She was happy and content in Maple Hills. She knew a life with Hawk would be fun and exciting, but she also knew she could count on him to make sure they had some quiet times like tonight. *He knows me so well*, she thought. She looked at the ring on her finger. Nikki took Hawk's hand in hers. She pulled him close and kissed him for a long time.

"What was that for?" he asked.

"For being one of the sweetest, kindest, gentlest human beings I know," she said. "I love you, Hawk, and I want to be with you for the rest of my life."

"I love you, too, Nikki. And I plan to be with you forever," Hawk replied, pulling her close. Their lips met again, and Nikki sighed. She knew she had finally found a man that truly made her happy. She smiled and pulled away.

"Last one to the kitchen is a rotten egg," she said, bounding away. Hawk laughed and followed her up the steps. The frogs around the lake serenaded their run, and the lake remained calm while the night owls screeched their hellos.

ABOUT THE AUTHOR

Wendy Meadows is the USA Today bestselling author of many novels and novellas, from cozy mysteries to clean, sweet romances. Check out her popular cozy mystery series Sweetfern Harbor, Alaska Cozy and Sweet Peach Bakery, just to name a few.

If you enjoyed this book, please take a few minutes to leave a review. Authors truly appreciate this, and it helps other readers decide if the book might be for them. Thank you! _

Get in touch with Wendy
www.wendymeadows.com

amazon.com/author/wendymeadows
goodreads.com/wendymeadows
bookbub.com/authors/wendy-meadows
facebook.com/AuthorWendyMeadows
twitter.com/wmeadowscozy

Made in the USA
Coppell, TX
01 February 2024

28470700R00061